Paper Crown

Paper Crown

a novel

JIM PETERSON

Red Hen Press 🐓 Los Angeles

Paper Crown

Cover art:
Hartley
Neel, Alice (American, 1900-1984)
Courtesy of National Gallery of Art, Washington

Book design by Michael Vukadinovich
Cover Design by Mark E. Cull
Cover Photo by Lyle Peterzell

ISBN: 1-59709-007-7

Library of Congress Catalog Card Number: 2004117569

Published by Red Hen Press

The City of Los Angeles Cultural Affairs Department, California Arts Council, Los Angeles County Arts Commission and National Endowment for the Arts partially support Red Hen Press.

First edition

For Jewelle and Harriet and Patti and Gayle
The Four Graces

Much gratitude to Kate Gale and Mark Cull

With thanks to Steve Corey, Gary Ferguson, and Marcos Villa-
toro for helpful readings of the manuscript

She doesn't dream
she knows
she is part of the pond she lives in,
the tall trees are her children,
the birds that swim above her
are tied to her by an unbreakable string.
　　　　　—Mary Oliver

. . . surely truth, if it exists for us to uncover in this world, is no dif-
ferent than a flood of light, out there for us to see but far more than
we can take in.
　　　　　—Peter Friederici

. . . they would look monstrous
If we could see them: the beautiful passionate bodies of living flame . . .
　　　　　—Robinson Jeffers

The old man stood up and stretched his hands toward heaven. His
fingers became like ten lamps of fire and he said, "If you will, you can
become all flame."
　　　　　—Joseph of Panephysis

In the dream of the man that dreamed, the dreamed one awoke.
　　　　　—Jorge Luis Borges

Chapter One

WHEN I WAS a very young man, I had nothing. It was okay to have nothing, but I didn't know that. There were so many things I thought I wanted. And then I met some people who made me believe I could have it all. Thirty years ago I lived in a small apartment in Colorado Springs, in an old building that should have been condemned. Every night I had this dream, more memory than dream:

The only sound was the air conditioner, sucking the sick air out through a filter, blowing the fresh, cool air in through small vents.

From a narrow opening in the curtains behind me, the moon and stars cast a pale column of light, my own shadow a series of smudged angles on the floor. I'd never felt this still, as if I were in a trance, my breath diminishing to something so small and automatic that it took all of my concentration to find it.

When the air conditioner went off, I could hear her breathing. The drugs would keep her under. I could see only the silhouette of her body under the sheet, but a small night light on the other side of her bed created little pockets of visibility. I could see the dust under her bed, the IV bottle dripping into the central line, more regular than her breathing.

My hands lay in my lap, half curled and limp. I could feel the slow, steady thump of pulse in my fingers. I couldn't sit here like this all night. There were things I had to do. But it felt good to be still and quiet and I didn't want to move. So I just sat, thinking and feeling almost nothing.

Suddenly, her breath caught and started again. Eyes opening, her head moved and raised a little. She blinked.

"Who is that? Charles?"

"Yes."

"Why aren't you home?"

"I wanted to stay here with you."

"All the others went home?"

"Yes."

She kept looking at me. She lifted her head farther and moved it from side to side as if she were trying to make something out.

"Where'd you get that paper crown?"

I put my hand on top of my head. My hair stood up from the way I'd been sleeping on it, and the light must have been shining through it strangely.

"Where'd you get it?" she said.

SOMEONE WAS KNOCKING on my door. I stayed in bed for a minute, trying to push the dream as far out of mind as I could. A dream as precise and durable as the watch my father had given me and which I kept in a drawer.

When I opened the door, Frank Posner walked past me without saying a word. There was something about the man that made me nervous. So I left the door open, just in case.

"Have a seat." I raked some dirty clothes from a chair, but Frank kept on standing. He looked around the room like he was studying, memorizing.

I didn't have many visitors. Dirty clothes were everywhere, paper cups and plates, and there wasn't a whole piece of furniture in the place, three legged things with cardboard boxes for a fourth.

"So you're Charles," he said.

"People call me Chuck."

"Do you still want a route, Charles?" He had short black hair and dark eyes with long black lashes like a girl's. He never looked me straight in the eye, but somewhere lower, maybe the mouth. I kept trying to engage his eyes, but never could.

"Yeah." I sat on the chair I'd cleared. "I need a job."

Frank unzipped his jacket half way, reached in and pulled out a pack of Winstons, tapped one out and lit it. I thought he would never get on with it, would never leave, like he was waiting for someone else to come in.

Then I noticed that the door was shut. It opened to the inside and no one but Frank had come in. There was no draft in that place. Hell, we were lucky we had air of any kind. But the door sure was closed, and it hadn't made a sound. I looked back at Frank who stood in the middle of the room, relaxed, smoking his cigarette, the ashes sizzling as he thumped them into a cup.

"Can you come down tomorrow?"

"Yeah."

"I'll meet you at the loading dock at one o'clock."

"Alright."

"Hey listen." Frank blew smoke through his nose. "You looking to stay a while, or you just fucking around?"

I gave him my meanest look.

"Just answer the question," Frank said, "I got three more names on the list."

"If I can make enough to pay the rent and eat, then I'll stay with it."

"You got another job?"

"Does it look like I got a job?"

"No, it doesn't. A lot of my people do though. It's just something I like to know."

"I ain't got time for two jobs. I got other things to do."

"Yeah, sure you do." Frank glanced around the room. "Listen, I got a new route on the map. It's a little tougher than the others, but you stand to make more money if you run it right. You interested?"

"Why not?"

Frank dropped the butt in the cup. The sizzling. "I'll show it to you tomorrow."

"I'll be there, one o'clock."

Frank zipped up his jacket, walked over and opened the door, and just as he was leaving looked back in. "Why don't you clean this shit up?" he said.

He was already out the door before I could come up with some kind of wise crack answer.

FROM THE FRONT, *The Sun*'s building was a sleek one-story with aspens standing on a landscaped lawn. But at the back where the carriers picked up their papers, it was four stories built into a steep slope. At one o'clock in the afternoon, the docking area of *The Sun* was crowded and busy. Pick-ups and vans played games of chicken to get those parking spaces at the front. I parked my Beetle out of the way and walked up a ramp onto the loading dock. There were three chutes feeding bundles of papers from an upper story down to where people worked away like ants on a slice of bread.

Frank came out of a door and walked to the edge of the dock, talking to a strong looking guy who was loading a truck. Frank laughed at something. He had this funny way of bouncing slightly on the balls of his feet. Finally he saw me and waved and came over. He seemed almost cheerful and not nearly so scary as the day before.

"Your papers will be on chute two," he yelled above the noise, pointing. "I had them work you into the first run. You should be able to pick them up by one o'clock every day."

Then he took me back to the office and showed me the computer print-out which had the paper count for the carriers each day. "This one's yours," he said, underlining the number 407 with his finger. The count was 317. He got me to sign an agreement with *The Sun*, setting me up as an individual businessman. I liked the sound of that. I would buy the papers at a low bulk rate from *The Sun*, then sell them at the much higher subscription rate. I should clear about a dollar per customer per month. Frank gave me two boxes of rubber bands and told me next time I would have to pay. He opened a drawer and pulled out a new pair of wire-cutters. "On the house," he said, tossing them to me.

Frank stopped long enough to light a Winston, then he led me up some stairs into the main part of the building where the giant presses were grinding out papers, and the newsroom where reporters were typing or talking on the phone. When we got back to the dock, the first run was coming to an end.

Frank found several bundles tagged 407 and had me bring in my car. We stacked the papers in the back seat and headed out. Frank explained that he had pieced this motor route together from several kids' bike routes. It was in a rough part of town and the kids were having a hard time collecting, so they had figured to solve the problem by bringing in an adult.

"If somebody don't pay you," Frank said, "just cut them out of the route. If they say something to you, tell them you'll start delivering as soon as they pay up what they owe you."

"How come that wouldn't work for the kids?"

Frank looked over at me, focusing from half-shut lids to somewhere below my eyes. "It would have if they could've done it. But there's some things it's hard for a kid to say to big people, because to them big people are like gods. Which is too bad, because it's the kids that really have it, like wizards, you know what I mean?" He tapped his forehead. "Up here."

I didn't know what he meant, and it wouldn't be the last time. "What do you mean, like wizards?"

Frank kept looking at me for a minute, focusing in that weird way, like a blind man who hears where someone is and looks at them in his mind. "Never mind," he said. "Take a left here. We start throwing in a couple of blocks."

While I was driving, Frank had been rolling papers, making good tight cylinders, which he dropped into a growing pile in the back seat.

"See that white house with the porch? That's where we start. Now pay attention. Slow down to fifteen."

He flipped a paper and the wind got under it like a frisbee and it sailed, then dropped lightly on the porch bouncing once, rolling up to the door. Frank grabbed another paper and hooked it over the top of the car. I caught sight of it slicing into the wind, and it dropped out into the middle of the yard across the street.

"Always drive slow enough to see where your paper lands," Frank said. "Some of these folks tip pretty good if you keep them happy."

For three long blocks, Frank kept on throwing papers to both sides of the street, talking the whole time. I was amazed at how he could throw, dropping that tight cylinder onto a porch or into the middle of a yard with the touch of a good outside shooting guard. When we came to a stop sign, Frank twisted around, looking back down the street.

"Do you think you can do that?"

"I guess so."

"Take a left."

Frank stuck his hand in his windbreaker and pulled out a sheet of paper with a list of addresses and notes about houses, but mostly he just kept rolling and throwing, or just rolling when there was a stretch without customers, so that he always had a good supply of papers ready to throw. He seemed to pay his hands no attention as they worked in front of him. He told me where to turn and pointed out each house, then threw the paper with pinpoint accuracy, keeping his eyes on it until it stopped rolling.

Then I saw something I couldn't believe. Frank flipped a paper toward a porch, but it came up short, slamming flat into the top step. But then it stood up on one end, walked up the step like some kind of cartoon character and rolled toward the door. All of a sudden my stomach sank like it does on a roller coaster and you're starting to head down, and I had to stop the car. Frank looked at me and just laughed.

"How the hell did you do that?"

"It's in the follow through." Frank showed me how to do it, stretching his arm out, letting his fingers flow out toward the target.

"That doesn't make any sense."

"If you really follow through," Frank went back to rolling papers, "it'll keep on going right where you want it."

I looked past Frank's head through the window to where the paper had stopped. An old woman opened the screen door and a small dog clamped down on one end of the paper and dragged it into the house.

"Let's go!" Frank slapped the steering wheel. "I ain't got all day."

We kept on this way for half an hour, then Frank said to park the car, and he showed me how to roll papers. He said that since this was Tuesday the papers were small and easy to roll and throw, but the Thursday and Sunday papers were sometimes two or three times bigger with extra pages of advertising and supplements and so on, and he'd have to show me how to handle those.

"I want you to show me how to throw," I said, but Frank ignored me.

We started up again with Frank driving this time and me rolling and throwing. Frank had to drive slow because I was so damn awkward rolling the papers. Also, we had to keep stopping to retrieve papers from under bushes and out of gutters. "Better short than sorry," Frank kept on saying. "If you break something, you pay for it." I managed to get one into a tree and Frank shook his head and laughed and stopped the car and we switched places again. It took us about three hours to complete the route. Frank had me driving like crazy through narrow alleys, through parking lots behind buildings, into driveways that had access to hidden passages. The route moved from neighborhoods with nice houses and their neat lawns, to motels that rented rooms by the month in the off season, oriental massage parlors, trailer parks, a fire station, an office building where we had to get out and carry the papers from floor to floor, and finally to broken-down houses on the outskirts of town where German shepherds lunged against fences, growling and barking.

When we finally got back to *The Sun*, Frank gave me a friendly punch on the arm. "You'll have it down pat in a couple of days. I'll see you tomorrow."

I wanted to punch him in the face, and probably would've, if I hadn't needed the job so bad.

FRANK WENT OUT with me for the next several days, experimenting with the route until we got it the way we wanted it. He showed me how to fold the big papers on Thursday and Sunday, how to double up on the rubber bands to hold them together, and to use the plastic bags *The Sun* provided for rainy days. But he was not interested in talking about his throwing techniques. After the first time out, I did all the throwing and started to develop my own style.

Every day I picked up my bundles from the dock, folded my papers in the parking lot, then went out on my route. On the weekends, *The Sun* was a morning paper, so I had to get my bundles around two a.m. It took me only about two hours to run the route, once I got it down, and the rest of the day was mine, which was the best thing about the job. At the end of each month I had to spend a couple of days collecting, but even that part didn't turn out to be the problem I thought it would, and several of my customers tipped me real good, which just about covered the ones who ran out on me. I was efficient, and it got to the point that I became attached to the route, to those particular people living in those particular homes, who depended on me to deliver the paper each day on cue like the sun in the morning and the moon at night. I was clearing over $300 a month, which not only covered my small living expenses, but left me enough to go out once in a while.

During that first year Frank kept an eye on me. I would throw the last bundle into the back seat of my Beetle and look up and there'd be Frank standing on the dock, cigarette in the corner of his mouth, hands behind his back or in his windbreaker pockets, rocking back and forth on his feet in that square stance. Sometimes I would snap to attention and salute and Frank would laugh and shake his head and disappear into his office.

Then I met Sandy.

Chapter Two

THE FIRST TIME I saw her was in a little bar around the corner from my apartment. She wore loose fitting jeans and a blue cotton shirt, so plain I didn't even notice her at first. She was next to me at the bar talking with the two girls she'd come in with. But when they turned to talk to two college boys, she straightened up and drank her beer slowly, as alone as I was. I let myself look at her and each time I looked, I looked longer. There was something about the way she dressed, the way she carried herself, that didn't invite you to look at her. But when you did, you realized she was beautiful. She stared into her glass, turning it around and around with her thumb and forefinger. I couldn't stop looking at her and began to search for something to say.

"Don't I know you from someplace?"

She glanced over at me, then looked back at her glass, shaking her head. "I don't think so."

"Do you come here much?"

"No."

"Listen, would you like to go for a ride or something?"

She looked back at me, one eyebrow slightly raised. Whenever I think of her now, that's what I see first, the way she raised her eyebrow on that first night.

I looked away, then back again. "I mean it's too loud in here to hear yourself think."

"I can hear you thinking." She smiled at me slyly.

"Is that a yes or a no?" I forced a laugh and tried to shrug the whole thing off.

She was so slow responding that I found myself just staring at her again. She looked at my hand, and it froze on the glass. I'd always hated my small, slender hands. "I guess it's a yes." She tapped the girl next to her, a red-head with lots of make-up who kept smiling and winking.

When we got out to the car, I turned on the radio, but kept it down low. I took her hand and introduced myself. She said her name was Sandy.

"Well, Sandy, where would you like to go?"

"Don't ask me. This was your idea."

"Jesus, we just met, and you already sound mad at me."

She took a deep breath and exhaled loudly. "I'm not mad at you. You've just caught me on a bad night, I guess."

"I was hoping that meeting me would make it a good night."

"I don't know why I'm telling you this. It's just that I lost my job. My roommates are kind of pissed off at me. Everything's just screwed up royally."

"Yeah, I know what you mean. I spend about half my life that way."

She smiled. "With an accent like that you must be from Georgia or Alabama."

"I thought I'd gotten rid of that."

"Sorry to pop your bubble."

"I'm from Rock Hill, South Carolina."

"What are you doing way out here?"

"Just staying away from back there I guess."

"That bad, huh?"

"Well, no, the place ain't that bad, if you like hot weather, pine trees and red clay. It was mainly, you know, the situation. My mother's been dead a while. My daddy and two older brothers, they're always older and wiser, always telling me how to live my life. I just got my fill of it and left. Been gone for three years."

She crossed her arms on her chest and leaned back against the door. "That must've been hard, just walking out like that. I don't see how you did it."

"It was pretty easy, once I'd made up my mind. What about you? Are you from around here?"

"Born and raised. Been here now for twenty-two years. Staying in one place so long makes you feel old. You know?"

"You don't look a day over twenty."

She laughed. "You don't have to try to say the right thing all the time."

"I wouldn't. I'm not like that."

"You don't look a day over twenty yourself."

I looked out my window. A man was lying on the sidewalk sound asleep, hands pressed together under his cheek, back flush against the dark bricks of an old wall. "I'm not."

"It's okay. You've got plenty of age in your eyes."

I didn't know what to say. I just felt young, like always. Too young to spit in the presence of real men, my father would say. "Do you want to go to my place? It's kind of a mess, but . . ."

"Why don't we go to my apartment?" she said. "It's all cleaned up and we could listen to records. My roommates won't be home for a while."

It sounded like a good plan to me. When we got to Sandy's place, she rolled a couple of joints, and we listened to Bob Dylan and Pink Floyd and talked for hours. I could not remember when I'd felt better. Sandy didn't take any bullshit, but still she was easy to talk to. I told her things I'd not told anyone since I'd left home. Things about living in my car, sleeping in truck stop parking lots and roadside parks, working at jobs I didn't even know existed, like cleaning out septic tanks. I didn't tell her everything, though. I didn't know her well enough for that.

When it got to be after one a.m., I roused myself. It was Saturday morning, and I had to go out on my route.

"Would you like to go with me? It's a really nice night for it."

She rolled another joint, catching all of the droppings on a sheet of typing paper then tapping them back into the baggie. I felt happy to have some company for a change. Around four o'clock we went to an all-nighter for breakfast. It was after five by the time I got her back home.

"Don't get out," she said. "Will you call me?" She raised an eyebrow, then leaned across and kissed me, just a little kiss.

But it was enough. I didn't think of anything but Sandy for days.

I WAITED THREE days before I called her. Didn't want it to seem like I was eager. But when she started going out with me, I had to struggle like an old boozer against a quart of Jim Beam not to ask her out every night. I struggled less and less, and we began to be together almost all the time. She was staying over with me two or three nights a week.

Then she started going on the route with me routinely. After all, it wasn't unpleasant to cruise around town for a couple of hours, playing the radio, talking, making plans for our date that night. The mechanics of rolling and throwing and driving were automatic for me by then. My body just did them. And Sandy made me more efficient by rolling some of the papers. I did my job well. My customers never complained.

But I could tell that Frank wasn't happy about something. When I introduced Sandy to him, Frank said, "Nice to meet you," and turned around and walked off. Every day Frank would watch me and Sandy loading up, but his look was stern, and almost sad. When I would snap to attention and salute, Frank wouldn't even change expression, just kept staring at me, smoking his Winston.

Then one day Frank called me into his office. He shut the door behind us, something he had never done before.

"What's up?" I said.

"We've got a little problem." Frank sat down and leaned back in his chair. "This girl you've been taking with you on the route . . ."

"What about it?"

"We don't like it." He stretched a rubber band between the thumb and forefinger of his right hand which was held out in the shape of a gun.

"I don't think it's any of your damn business." I caught myself balling both hands into fists. I tried to let them relax.

"Don't get smart with me," Frank said, and the rubber band slipped off his thumb and popped against the wall next to me. I couldn't take my eyes off it. It was squirming against the wall like some kind of crazed insect. Finally, it fell to the floor, and when I looked back at Frank, my stomach felt just like that rubber band. Frank's eyes were dilated, round as bullet holes, the thin whites giving them a shimmery focus.

"I pay for my papers, don't I?" My voice shook like a choirgirl's talking to the preacher.

Frank nodded. "I ain't worried about that."

"Well what then?"

"We don't want you getting distracted. The customers come first."

"Have you had any complaints from my customers?"

Frank shook his head. "Don't want none either."

"When you start getting complaints, let me know. In the meantime, nobody tells me what to do." During my three years on the road, I'd learned how to act tough, even when I was scared out of my wits.

Frank picked up another rubber band from the pile on his desk. "You don't want us to get unhappy with you, now do you?"

I was mad and afraid, and I didn't like either one of those feelings. I started inching toward the door. "Look," I said, "you may not believe it but I can read, and there ain't nothing on that agreement I signed that says I can't have somebody riding with me, as long as I do my job. Besides, every other carrier I know has somebody riding with him."

Another rubber band shot across the room, flew by my ear and stuck on the wall, wiggling like a chunk of butter on a frying pan. "Just family," Frank said. "They don't have a whore riding with them."

That was more than I could take, and I started toward him. For the first time since I had known him, Frank looked me dead in the eyes. It was like a snake slipped inside of me and sank its teeth in my guts. It stopped me in my tracks. The frustration I felt made me even madder, but I couldn't move.

Frank stood up slowly and put his hands out in front of him like he was pushing something away. "I'm sorry," he said casually. "I didn't mean that." He moved his eyes away and I almost fell, caught myself against the desk. I did my best to glare at Frank. His eyes no longer quite met mine, but focused somewhere lower, and seemed to be getting back to normal.

I was suddenly tired and out of breath, though I'd barely moved a muscle. "I don't know if this job is worth so much trouble. If you don't like the way I do it, then fire me."

"Okay, I'm sorry." Frank made that pushing-away motion with his hands again. "I got out of line. I just thought I'd warn you, that's all."

"A warning?"

"I'm only looking out for you."

"You'd better just look out for yourself."

I slammed the door behind me. I was shaking so hard I could barely walk. Sandy was waiting for me at the car with the back seat loaded up. I looked at her standing there in those baggy jeans and her long brown hair and not a dot of make-up on her, and I wondered how anybody could think she was a whore. For the first time in a long time, I felt afraid and unhappy. I couldn't figure out what Frank was after, why he was behaving the way he was, or how he was able to do those things with the rubber bands. And what was going on with his eyes? "Why is he bothering me?" I kept on asking myself.

I FINALLY HAD to admit that I was in love with Sandy. She was a few years older, but that didn't matter. After she lost her job as a secretary, her roommates began to be unhappy about having to cover her share of the rent and utilities. They didn't exactly kick her out, because they were her friends, or said they were, but she was feeling some pressure, so she just moved in with me.

She was the first girl I ever really slept with, and she kept me turned on all the time. Every time I walked by she grabbed me, and every time she walked by I grabbed her, and we just got to where we didn't go out all that much. I found out that if we were careful it didn't cost the two of us any more to live than it had cost me to live by myself. Sometimes she would come up with a little money to help out, but I never was quite sure where she'd got it from. Generally, there had never been a time in my life when I felt better, more complete, than I felt then. Everything was in its place, and there was just enough of everything to get by, and Sandy and I were so tight we could just look at each other and know what the other one was thinking.

My only problem was with Frank.

One day when Sandy and I had finished the route, she still had a stack of fifteen papers in her lap. The next day I braved Frank's office, which was empty. I checked the print-out and sure enough the number had been jacked up, so I cut it back to just what I needed, plus a couple extra for myself, and to be safe. But the next day I ran fifteen papers over again. Somehow my cut had not been registered on the print-out, so I cut it back again. But I kept on running into the same problem, always ten to fifteen papers over. This wouldn't have bothered me so much except that I was paying for those extra papers, and that could cost me fifteen to twenty bucks a month. I put it off as long as I could, but finally I had to go see Frank about it.

It took me a few days, but I finally caught Frank in his office.

"Come in. What can I do for you?" Frank leaned back in his chair and put his feet up on the desk. His eyelids were red, and he kept rubbing them.

I took a deep breath. "Look, I keep running way over on my papers every day. I cut the number back, but the message ain't getting through upstairs."

Frank leered at me, an expression I didn't think was possible for his face. He spoke quietly. "I'll take care of it. Everybody's pushing, you know, to keep those numbers up. Keeping the pressure on. I'll check it out."

"Thanks," I said. Then I went over to the print-out and cut the number back to what I needed again, and started out.

"Hey Chuck," Frank called, "how's your supply?" He stood up and pointed to the stack of rubber band boxes in the corner.

"I'm doing okay."

He grabbed a box and tossed it over to me. I didn't need it right then, but I knew I could use it later, so I reached in my pocket.

Frank shook his head. "It's on the house. You been doing a good job. Just, you know, a token to let you know. Now get out of here before anybody gets any ideas."

"What do you mean?"

"Forget it. I'll take care of the cut. Now get out of here."

So I got out.

But the situation didn't get any better. For the next three days I ran over just as much as before. So I sat down that night and figured out how much *The Sun* owed me. The next day I went in to see Frank again. I found him leaning against one of the chutes on the dock. He was smoking a Winston and watching the carriers line up for the first run. When he saw me, he glanced at his watch.

"Kind of early ain't you?"

"I need to talk to you."

"I'm listening."

"In private."

Frank took a drag from his cigarette, dropped it on the concrete floor and stepped on it, taking an extra few seconds to grind it in with a twisting motion of his foot. I followed him into his office and shut the door. Frank sat down in the squeaky chair, crossed his feet up on the desk, and clasped his hands behind his head.

"Okay, so what's the problem?"

There was something too casual in Frank's movements, like someone idly whistling.

"It's the same problem, Frank. Too many papers. I thought you said you were gonna take care of that for me."

"I thought I had."

"Why are you fucking around with me?"

Frank grinned and chuckled. "Nobody's fucking around, Chuck."

"The more papers go out, the better you look upstairs. That's right, ain't it?"

"Yeah, that's right." Frank reached inside his jacket to his shirt pocket. He pulled out his pack of Winstons, shook one up, took it out and tapped it on his thumbnail. "Is that all?"

"No, that ain't all."

"Well, get on with it."

"All I know is, somebody's stealing from me, and it's probably you. You can kick me off the route if you want, but I'm not gonna let you steal from me."

Frank shook his head and laughed again. It was a low grumbly laugh like nothing in the world could touch him. He lit the cigarette.

"My contract says I got the right to order the number of papers I need. I can't afford to pay for a bunch of extra papers just to make you look good."

Frank chuckled again and shook his head. "Do you really think a few extra papers is gonna make me look better with those boys upstairs?"

"I don't know. A little here and a little there adds up."

"Jesus, what a fucking dumbass."

"I'm not gonna pay for those papers."

"That bitch must have her hooks right into your pockets."

I couldn't believe I'd heard him say that. I was so stunned I just stood there for a minute with my mouth open. Finally, I measured out some words. "I think it's pretty strange you're so damn interested in my love life."

"Now why would I be interested in *that*?"

"You tell me. I just don't like the way you talk about her. And if you keep on I'm gonna have to hurt you."

Frank laughed his raspy smoker's laugh and leaned forward in his chair. "And how do you think you could hurt me?"

"I could go up and talk to Mr. Holloway about how you got this weird thing about my girlfriend. He might not want to take the chance of having somebody like that on the team."

"Jesus, you talk big for a kid that doesn't know a damn thing about anything. But don't worry, that won't be necessary." He took out his wallet and pulled out a ten.

"Will this cover it?"

"It's close enough."

I'd been waiting for Frank to pull one of his weird stunts, and he didn't disappoint me. He reached the bill out toward me and let it go. I figure you're not going to believe what I'm about to say. I'm just telling you what happened. That bill stayed suspended in the air between us. Frank was laughing again, blowing smoke through his nose.

"How the hell do you do that?"

"Do what?" Frank shrugged his shoulders, wide-eyed.

I reached out but the bill slipped away.

"Do you do this bit for everybody, or just for me?"

"Just for you," Frank said slowly.

"Do I get the money or not?"

"Yeah, you get it."

The bill wadded itself into a ball, jumped into my face and fell on the floor. Frank got up and walked to the door. He bumped me with his shoulder as he went by me. I felt like I was back in high school, all that testosterone. He turned and looked at me.

"Anything else?"

I gave him my best squint. Back then I was always trying to look mean. "No, you're such a nice guy Frank, I don't want anything from you. No wonder you're by yourself all the time." It was the worst insult I could think of.

Frank's eyes darkened and shifted straight into mine. That scared the shit out of me and I took a step back. But all I felt was a pressure against my eyes, like fingertips. Then Frank was gone.

I stood there in his office, a little stunned, extremely alert, like something important had just happened. But what was it? In Frank's absence, the office, which was so vibrant and threatening when he was there, now seemed dingy and pathetic. His desk was littered with the tiny, lifeless serpents of broken rubber bands. A note was tacked on the bulletin board behind Frank's desk. I stepped sideways deeper into the office hearing the grit crack under my shoes. Nervous about the idea of going behind Frank's desk, I leaned across it. I could tell the scrawl of the writing was not a result of the writer's being in a rush, but that it was designed to be hard to read. Just two words. Suddenly I could decipher their screwball script: *REMEMBER YOURSELF.*

I DID MY best to avoid Frank after that, but for those few minutes every day at the loading dock I felt like I was haunted. I never let my eyes come to rest on Frank. But I felt him there, rocking back and forth from heel to toe in that square stance, smoking, following me with those dark, lazy eyes.

I hadn't told Sandy about the real problem, only that Frank and I were not on good terms right now. But she was at *The Sun* with me every day, and she could sense there was more to it. I decided to tell her about Frank's strange abilities, but not about his attitude towards her. I didn't want to upset her, or get her involved in some way. After all, it was between me and Frank. One afternoon I told her all the strange things I'd seen Frank do, and about his weird eyes. She just shook her head and laughed.

"You're really letting this guy get under your skin, aren't you?"

"I guess I am."

"You can't let him walk all over you."

I sat up in my chair. "I didn't!"

"I know, I know." She came around behind me, working her hands inside the neckline of my shirt, massaging. I could feel the tension draining off into her fingers, and I closed my eyes.

"I just don't like to see somebody intimidate you."

"Well if you saw him in action you might be intimidated too."

"It sounds to me like he knows a few magic tricks, that's all. I know too much science to believe in that kind of thing. I was a physics major for a while."

"It wasn't no magic trick." I shook my head slowly. "It was for real."

"I don't know. I've seen magicians do weirder stuff than that on TV plenty of times."

I twisted around to look at her. "Yeah, but that's on TV. Frank didn't have hidden wires, or mirrors, or trick photography." I turned back around and she went on massaging.

"How do you know he didn't?"

"Because I was there and I didn't see anything like that."

"But if they were hidden, then you wouldn't have seen them."

"Ouch," I said, "take it easy. I didn't see them because they weren't there. There's no way he could set that up except on a stage. I'm telling you, he did it with his eyes."

"With his eyes."

"I know it sounds crazy, but that's how he did it."

Sandy flopped down across from me, legs draped over one arm of the chair. "Well if he upsets you so much, why don't you look for another job? You could make more money and probably get the weekends off. We could drive up into the mountains and spend a couple of nights under the stars."

I didn't move. I wanted to calm myself before I said anything. It was always hard for me to talk about money. "If you're worried about more money, then why don't *you* look for a job? You're the one with all those college credits. I don't have anything now and odds are I won't ever have anything. You know that, so you might as well get used to it, or start looking for someone else."

Sandy knelt down in front of me, hugging my knees. "You know I don't want anyone else. And I don't care anything about the money. I just don't like to see you unhappy. I thought maybe a change would help."

I stroked her hair, cool and silky between my fingers. She looked so straight into my eyes I had to smile. "You might be right. I've just got to think about it some." I shook my head. I didn't want to say anything else. I didn't want to do anything to screw up the best relationship I'd ever had. Hell, the only complete relationship with a woman I'd ever had.

"Except for Frank I'm happier now than I've ever been," I said.
"Me too." She crawled into my lap.

Chapter Three

I STARTED GETTING the right number of papers again. For the next six weeks I rarely saw Frank, who no longer stood over our position at the dock and watched us. I was relieved, but I always looked to see if he was there, somewhere, among the workers on the dock.

Now that things were getting back to normal, I decided not to think about another job. I still liked the free time the route gave me, and the fact that it ran so smooth. And I enjoyed the different kinds of people I met, the retirees, the middle-aged hard-nosed workers, the young couples with a baby on the way, even the down-and-out ramblers like myself in their rented rooms, whose lives I got a glimpse of waiting in a foyer while they went to get their money. Besides, it would have been too much trouble to make a change.

But one afternoon Frank reappeared at his old spot above us on the dock. He motioned for me to follow him to the office.

He didn't look so good. There were circles under his eyes and he had lost weight. In a motion so practiced it was nearly invisible, he sat down and propped his feet up on the desk. I waited. I had nothing to say. I would just keep on waiting. Frank rubbed his eyes, then laughed softly.

"You've done real good, you know that?" He grinned.

"I do the best I can."

"You don't even know what I'm talking about, do you?"

I nodded. "The route."

He shook his head almost sadly, squinting his eyes as he shifted them squarely into mine. I felt that strange touch on my eyes at first, then on my face. I covered my face and felt it like the nibbling of small fish on the backs of my hands.

"Listen," Frank said. "You can stop being afraid of me. All that's over with."

"Who said I'm afraid?"

"Some things are obvious."

"Sandy's waiting on me." I took a step back. "Is this little meeting necessary?"

"Yes, it is," Frank said.

I grabbed the doorknob, ready to get out of there fast.

"We need to get together," Frank continued. "We have some important things to discuss." He lit up a cigarette.

I paused, but didn't take my hand off that door. "Like what?"

"Like your future for example."

"What's that got to do with you?"

"Nothing." Frank blew smoke through that word. "That's why we've got to talk about it now."

The doorknob wouldn't turn.

"I just don't have anything to say to you, Frank."

"But suppose I have something to say to you."

"Like what?"

Frank grinned. "Let's just say I want to talk to you about *this*."

I felt a light slap across my cheek. Frank was fifteen feet away, sitting in his chair, that grin still pasted on his face like he'd just won the state lottery or something. Then he wrote something on a slip of paper and brought it to me.

"I live just a little ways from here. Call me if you can't come. But come. It's important. Seven sharp, tonight."

I looked at the piece of paper. "I'm not sure I can make it."

"How come? Won't your wife let you have a night out with the boys?"

I looked into those strange, laughing eyes. This time, there seemed to be no malice in them. "I'll just have to see." I slid the paper into my wallet.

SANDY WAS FOLDING papers and throwing them into the back seat when I got in.

"Did he give you a hard time?"

"Not really. He wants me to come see him at his place. Tonight."

"Aha!" she said, raising her eyebrow.

I shook my head. "Nah. I don't think Frank's gay."

"You don't think?"

"He wants to talk about those things he does."

"Did he show you any more of his tricks?" She laughed.

"Sort of. He kept on touching my face. Only he was on the other side of the room."

"This guy is sounding weirder all the time. You gonna go?"

"I've got to find out how he does it."

"Am I invited?"

I gave her my what-do-you-think expression.

"It figures." She slam dunked a rolled paper into the back seat.

"Now don't get bent out of shape. You two don't get along anyway."

"How do you know? We've never said more than two words to each other."

"You'd just think his tricks are dumb and make fun of him. Besides, they probably *are* dumb and I won't stay long anyway."

She stretched a rubber band across her thumb and forefinger. It hit the side of my head and stuck in my hair. "Hey," I said, "do you want to start a war?" Rubber band wars were not uncommon. I noticed a shade of resentment in her eyes.

"Do you really want to go?"

"No. Let's talk about something else."

IT WAS A small white house in a row of small white houses, and the yellow light over the front door was on. Frank led me to the living room and to two large, comfortable lounge chairs that were separated by a small end table with a slender lamp. He left the room, saying he'd be right back. The house was simply furnished and extremely neat. There was a couch with afghans, another chair and a book case, a couple of still life paintings on the wall, forest scenes, along with a photograph of a tuxedoed older gentleman with a partially white beard and a somewhat younger woman. Her blouse was wrinkled and haphazardly buttoned, open at the throat, collar standing up on one side of her face and down on the other. She had a pleasant, wide-eyed expression with a generous, unaffected smile, but I could see that the old man was the origin of Frank's eyes, dark and penetrating with those long lashes like a girl's. The woman's arm was not visible, but her hand appeared on the table in front of her like something separate with a life of its own. Her hair was straight and black and long, her skin dark compared to the man's.

Frank returned with two cans of beer and two glasses and set them on the table. "You drink beer?"

I nodded. "How come you're being so nice all of a sudden?"

"I'm not really as big an asshole as you think. All those things I said and did had a reason. I had to find out how you'd react."

I couldn't stay still in my chair. I wanted to be calm, or at least to look calm, but I was so curious and nervous I was about to explode. "So did I pass the test?"

"You did real good. You showed a fighting spirit, and you stayed pretty relaxed in strange circumstances. Those things'll come in handy. They're not the best, but they're good. They'll get you started."

"Started on what?"

"I'm going to tell you. Later."

"What would be the best?"

"The best would be hollowness. But that's rare. I've never met a person who was completely hollow right at the start."

"But why would anybody want to be hollow, whatever that means?"

"That's a good question. I think you'll find out for yourself."

I shook my head. I didn't have the foggiest idea what he was talking about.

"Don't worry about it," he said. "We'll talk about that later. What I really want to talk about tonight is 'making contact.'"

"I don't understand *anything* you're saying."

"You know those things you saw me doing in my office? That's what we call 'making contact.'"

"We?"

"There are others."

"And you want to make me one of them."

"I can't make you anything."

"And what if I don't want to?"

"Then you can go on about your business." Frank took out a cigarette.

"Well, it doesn't look like I have anything to lose, does it?"

"I didn't say that."

"So there's a catch."

"Yeah." He blew smoke, gazing up through it to the ceiling. "There's a catch, but I can't tell you what it is, mainly because it's different for everybody. For some people it doesn't amount to very much. For other people it's worse than dying. It's just a risk you'll have to take."

Everything Frank said seemed calculated, extreme, even melodramatic. A part of me wanted to laugh out loud at him, but I held it back. "What makes you think I'm gonna take a chance like that, especially when I don't know what the hell you're talking about?"

"I don't have any idea what you're gonna do. I'm just giving you an option. But let me ask you something. How much education do you have?"

"Not much." I looked at my right hand, at the paper cut in the valley between my thumb and forefinger.

"How much?"

"Half way through the tenth grade."

Frank nodded and grinned, letting go of more smoke through his teeth. "Good. Your head isn't so crammed full of education you think you know everything. And, you don't have a lot of strong attachments."

"These are good things?"

"In my world. Yes."

"You make it sound like your world is different from this world, *my* world."

"There is only one world. But each of us claims a part of it, don't we? That's all I meant."

I slumped back in my chair like I used to do when my mother was alive, when I wanted to frustrate her attempts to talk to me. We were silent for a while. I felt a long way from home, a long way from Sandy. I was tired and jittery, but my curiosity wanted more. I wanted to ask a question that would begin to get a real answer from Frank.

"So how did you get started with all of this?"

"I had all the advantages." Frank smiled, thumping ashes into his empty beer can. "Only I blew it for a long time. I was like the son of a rich man that takes everything for granted because he has everything, and becomes a lazy fool." He stubbed out his cigarette and cocked his head at the photographs on the wall. "Those are my parents. My father was a magician . . ."

This time I did laugh aloud. "So it was just magic tricks. That's what Sandy said all along."

"Not so goddamn fast." Frank looked at the pictures. "My mother is a psychic." He looked at me, expecting an outburst. I stayed quiet this time. He nodded and went on. "They made quite a team. My father was a real magician's magician, gave his whole life to magic and illusion. Could do things with his hands that would just make you want to cry when you realized how much time and pain it had cost him. Stuff was always appearing and then disappearing into thin air. His hands were big, but he could make them small by dislocating the joints. The same with his shoulders. Handcuffs and straight jackets were a joke to him."

I looked at my hands. Artist's hands, my mother always said, slim and graceful. But I had never been an artist. I couldn't draw worth a damn and I never learned anything about music. I thought about deliberately dislocating my thumb joints just to make my hands smaller. I imagined slipping them through those metal rings.

Frank continued. "As a performer he was not great. I mean he was okay, he was good enough to make a living, but he was more interested in doing the trick than dazzling the audience. His performances were kind of quiet and smooth."

Now I watched Frank's hands as he removed another cigarette from the pack. Like many chronic smokers, his work with a cigarette was an unconscious performance, as quiet and smooth, I was willing to bet, as any of his father's tricks. The cigarette seemed to have an energy of its own as it flicked among his fingers, until it finally conducted the smoke into his throat.

"So anyway, I spent a lot of time as a kid traveling around with my parents from town to town with this troupe of magicians and comedians. My father was by far the best magician of the bunch, even if he wasn't the main attraction. The other magicians were always getting him to help them with some technique, some illusion for their act."

Frank waved his hand in the air. I expected his cigarette to disappear.

"There was this one guy you wouldn't believe. It was just after World War II, and he looked more like Hitler than Hitler did. He had the little mustache and the slicked back hair and those cold, beady eyes. His wife was his stage assistant. Terrific looking, especially in that skimpy outfit she wore. The act was built around the magician as a villain, and the beautiful girl was always caught in the villain's trap, about to be sawed in half or drowned or levitated over a bed of steel spikes and all kinds of dangerous things, only she always managed to outsmart the villain by disappearing and then reappearing in a safe place. The audience would go wild. It was the craziest thing you ever saw. The magician was really just about as nice a guy as you'd ever meet, always sitting around with my father, picking up on new ideas."

I began to relax. The more I listened to Frank's voice, the less threatening he was. I realized that even if I didn't ask any questions, he was going to tell me his story. But I did ask. I wanted to hear him talk, even if it was all a lie. "Did your father teach you how to do those things?"

"He tried to teach me, and I learned a little, but not as much as I should've. I just wouldn't put in the time. It's like learning how to play the piano, only harder I think. It takes a lot of practice. I was too busy looking at the girls and just generally trying to figure out what was going on, you know?"

"Yeah, I know."

"It was my mother who caused everything to change." He put his cigarette out, half smoked, and pulled out another. "She was the one who planted the seed, the idea that he could do his illusions with a part of himself he wasn't even aware of."

Frank sat forward in his chair now, this expounding on his mother and father bringing new energy to his eyes and face, too involved in his subject to light his cigarette for the moment.

"There were things he could do that none of the other magicians could ever pull off, no matter how hard they tried, even after he'd told them how it was done. He was a generous man that way, gave away every idea or technique he ever came up with. Some of the others were decent guys and gave him credit, but a lot of them didn't. He didn't care. Never heard him say a word about it or react in any way. That was another advantage I had. My father was a very hollow man. Never held anything back for himself, and so you couldn't hurt him, you know?"

I nodded, but I didn't know.

"Always had everything he wanted. He just loved magic. Doing it, thinking about it, talking about it."

He sat back in his chair now and smiled. "But my mother's idea started changing things for him. My father was Benjamin Fallaw, son of a Kansas farmer. He took up magic because his life on the farm was boring. Ran away from home when he was fifteen or sixteen and by the time he was twenty had his own magic side-show that traveled with a small circus. Everywhere he went he would find the best magicians and learn what he could from them. By the time he met my mother many years later, he was a master magician, the best of the best. But he was pretty much unknown and had very little money while third rate magicians like Houdini had become rich and famous. But Houdini had something special and my father was the first to admit it. When he was still a young magician in his teens and twenties, he met with Houdini a number of times and considered him a friend. He loved that strong little man. He said that Houdini had a simple graciousness about him that you could feel all the way across the room before the man had said a word. It was a terrible and unnecessary thing, the way he died so young. My father was in the audience that very night, the night that Houdini didn't make it to the stage."

Finally he paused to light up and blew out a thoughtful white cloud.

"Now my mother is a different story altogether. Lyuba is the only name I've ever heard her use. My father used to call her 'Plum' and sometimes 'Plumcake,' but that was his privilege. She was a daughter of the chief of a tribe of nomads called the Lowara. The many tribes of these people taken together call themselves the Rom. We call them Gypsies. They roam practically every part of the world with very little regard for the boundaries, laws or customs of the so-called developed cultures. They trace their roots back to a place before names, to a time before laws. According to my mother, it was there and then they learned the ways of the Sun from a race of people that has since disappeared from the planet. Even the Lowara people have no stories in their oral tradition to tell them what these teachers were like. They only know that they were powerful but gentle beings who wanted to share their understanding. Their insights and powers have been passed on in secret from generation to generation of the Lowara people since that time."

I had to give Frank credit. He could tell a good story. I looked at the photograph of his parents. There was an incongruity between the two, the spiffy theatrical gentleman and the slightly disheveled darker woman, as if someone had somehow spliced two separate photos together to give the appearance of one.

"My mother is one of the few women to ever leave that tribe," Frank said. "The paths of my father's traveling show and my mother's people coincided for a period of several weeks, and she fell in love with him. My mother says he was a strong, beautiful man whose extreme reserve was a great challenge to her. For the Lowara, sexual love is a calling that should never be denied. This doesn't mean they are a promiscuous people. But they believe that when a person really falls, they have to follow. It was all made easier by the fact that my father led a nomadic life that was not that different from her own. And his hollowness was the very quality of her people that had attracted the original teachers to them in the first place. He had no expectations of her. She continued with the routineless lifestyle of her people and he loved her for it. She set herself up as a psychic and spiritual medium so she could be part of my father's show, but that was just a game to make a little extra money. Her powers were different, and far greater than that, and she kept them to herself.

"Until one day she started teaching them to my father. The time came when he could do a lot of his old illusions without the usual mechanical gimmicks or physical maneuvering. He could just do them. Well this blew his mind because it was the physical discipline he'd always loved so much, and counted on. But Lyuba had things under control. She'd been preparing him for this for years without him even knowing it, preparing him for the same thing I've been preparing you for, the thing I'm going to show you tonight."

He looked at me and smiled. I felt a gentle probing of my face. My stomach sank a little, but I stayed calm, beginning to realize that this contact was nothing to be afraid of. It was Frank, or some part of Frank, reaching out to me. I didn't know if this "touching" had romantic implications, as Sandy suspected, but I didn't believe it did.

"But how can you show me?" I asked. "I'm not ready for it. I don't know anything about it."

"You know more than you think." Frank raked his black hair back on his head. He seemed perpetually tired to me. "The body has to be prepared for these things, or else the shock could fuck it up, maybe even kill it. It can only take small doses to start with, then more and more. I started giving you small doses over a year ago. That's when I found out how tough you are. I've been reaching down into you and shaking you up a good bit, and you just keep on getting stronger."

"I don't like all this screwing around with my head. Makes me feel like I'm being brain-washed or something."

"It was the only way. You might have put up a defense if you'd known, like some people do when they go to the doctor. Then nothing could have been done." He sat up straight in his chair and looked at me. "Well, are you ready?"

"I don't think I am." I wiped the sweat from my upper lip. "I don't feel so good."

Frank laughed. "Don't worry about it. You're ready. I've made sure of that."

FRANK MADE ME sit on the couch. My line of sight was at a right angle to his.

"Now just relax and clear your mind and keep your eyes open."

He switched off the lamp. Curtains made a tight seal over the window, there were no other lights on in the house, and it was already dark outside. The living room was pitch black. For a moment I couldn't see or hear anything.

Almost immediately I began to feel tired and sleepy and had to work hard to make myself keep staring into the darkness. But for a long time there was not a sound or a movement. Then I saw something flash, like a flashbulb, only it was quicker. This woke me up and my eyes stung with the strain of looking so hard into the darkness. Then there was the flash again and it was slower and I could see it better. It seemed to lunge from the point where Frank was sitting, and stretched out across the whole room, then was pulled back, almost snapped back, to Frank. I waited for it to happen again, only I wasn't sure that my stomach could take it. I was breathing heavily out of my mouth by now, but I couldn't catch my breath.

This time, I could feel it moving in my body before I could see it, as if it were coming from both of us, not just Frank. It was forcing its way out of something, like a larva working free of its cocoon. Then it shot across the room, a silent explosion, very bright light only it didn't hurt my eyes. It had form, wagging lazily in front of me like a cat's tail, a splash of luminescence attached to my stomach by smaller threads of light. I stared so hard and long that it looked like a giant fish steadying itself against a stream. Then it began to slide back and into the darkness as if it were being swallowed. The threads of light pulled harder on my stomach and my head was spinning with nausea. The threads kept pulling at my insides, and I vomited. I crashed forward onto the coffee table and then onto the floor. I looked up and saw the huge shape of the light slowly inserting itself back into the dark lump of Frank's body which I could now barely make out. I grabbed one of the threads with both hands and it was like very cold wire. It pulled me, stumbling, towards Frank. My knees buckled and I went back down at his feet. He was speaking to me, only there was no sound. I felt these words in my own body as if they were coming from myself. "Remember yourself," it kept on saying. This was all that I could hear or remember for a long time.

MY CLOTHES WERE still damp, my body cool in the draft from an open window, and there was a wet cloth on my forehead. On a bed-side table a portable radio played "Down in the Boondocks" softly.

"Welcome back," Frank said from a nearby chair. "How do you feel?"

"Weak, tired."

"You ought to be tired after that fight you put up in there."

"What did you do to me?" I raised up on an elbow.

"Not a thing."

"And that's what your mother showed your father?"

Frank nodded. "Of course the situation was a lot different. He was already close to making the discovery for himself, using the hints she'd been giving him for years."

"Well why did it have to beat the shit out of me?"

"It didn't. You did that to yourself."

"Yeah, sure." I flopped back down on the bed. "I'm sorry if I screwed up."

"You didn't screw up. This stuff isn't easy. It takes time." He got up and left the room.

"Why do I have to get used to it?" I yelled.

"You don't," Frank called back. "But I figure you will."

"How come?"

"Because it's in your blood now. How can you go on and just ignore what you saw tonight?"

Frank came back in with a glass of water and handed it to me. I took a long drink, watching Frank over the glass as he sat down.

"But I don't really know what it was I saw." I wiped my mouth with the back of my hand.

"You saw my light."

"Does everybody have light inside like that?"

"Yeah, but knowing it's there and taking control of it are two different things."

This was all happening too fast, too easy. I don't think I was ready to believe anything Frank said, but I had to play along. "Do you think I could learn?"

"I don't know for sure. Do you want to try?"

I thought about it for about five seconds. "I think I do. When can we start?"

"Not so fast. You've got to recover from this first. I'll let you know, don't worry."

"And what kind of light has physical properties like that . . . you know . . . that you can touch and manipulate?"

"Maybe it isn't light at all."

Was that all he could say? I finished the glass of water and set it down. "Is your mother still alive?"

"Yes." Frank leaned toward me. "She's alive. Is your mother still alive?"

Suddenly, I felt I would choke if I tried to speak. It seemed like a strange question since I hadn't mentioned my mother in any conversation with him.

Frank finally got up from his chair and motioned to me. "Come on. It's getting late. You don't want Sandy to get mad do you?"

"Don't start in on me." I dragged myself up.

He crawled into the bed behind me and let go of a deep breath. "Jesus, I'm tired."

He fell asleep before I was out of the room, Mick Jagger singing "Ruby Tuesday" in the background.

I CREPT INTO bed beside Sandy as quietly as I could, but she woke up and rolled over to face me. She draped her arm around my neck and pulled me close.

"Your body's so cool."

"Yeah, it's kind of cool out."

"What took you so long? I was waiting up but I got too sleepy."

"That's okay. It just took longer than I thought."

"Did he do any of his tricks?"

"Sort of."

"And you were impressed I bet."

"You'd be impressed too if you'd seen it." I described what had happened. She didn't think about it long.

"It was a trick."

"No way."

"Mirrors. Why do you think he made it so dark in there?"

"Well that doesn't explain the physical stuff, the way I was pulled off the couch and everything."

"A lot of things can happen when it's that dark."

"That doesn't make any sense."

"And you think Frank's explanation makes sense? All that stuff about having a big fish ray or something inside of us just waiting to express itself?"

"Maybe not. But I know what I saw. And there were no mirrors and no tricks." I realized for the first time that I did believe Frank, that his demonstration had convinced me.

She was silent for a while. "I'm really starting to worry about this business with Frank."

"You shouldn't."

"But just look at it. First he pulls all that crap down at the paper, trying to steal from you and all. Now it's all this weirdo magic. I mean, what does he want from you?"

"Nothing."

"I just didn't think you could be so gullible."

"But that's the point. I've never been gullible."

She groaned. "You are like the Ace of Gullible."

"Believe me, whatever Frank is, he's not a phony."

"But how do you know? You don't know anything about him."

"I know he's kept his job at *The Sun* for a lot of years. I know his father was one of the best magicians in the world, and his mother's a psychic."

There was another long silence. I could feel her double-taking in the darkness.

"I rest my case," she said.

"I rest mine too, because I can't really prove anything to you."

"Listen to me," she said. Her voice seemed small, seemed to come out of a distant cave in the darkness. "Those three years I was in college, I was studying science, trying to decide between biology and physics. I was good at it Chuck. I know a lot of stuff. And I'm telling you, light doesn't behave the way Frank says it does, the way you described it. It just doesn't. Okay?"

"I thought you'd rested your case," I said.

"I thought I had too," she said. "I guess time will tell which one of us is crazy." She snuggled close against me. Her hand moved along my thigh, cupped me playfully. When she didn't get the response she'd hoped for, she rolled away. "Jesus, he didn't suck your blood or anything, did he?"

I forced myself to laugh. "No, it was just kind of strenuous."

"Now I'm really worried, if he's gonna have this kind of effect on you."

"You don't have to worry about that." I moved my hand up between her thighs until I touched her. I put my other arm around her, kissing her, starting to make love to her with my hand. But she pulled it away and turned over.

"Not like that," she said. "Let's get some sleep."

Chapter Four

BUT SANDY WAS right to believe that first visit with Frank had had a strong effect on me. I wanted to talk to Frank about it, but he didn't seem interested. In fact, Frank could no longer be found at *The Sun* during the time that I was there. He'd started taking his lunch at that hour. I called him at home, but never got an answer. A month went by, and I gradually settled back into the routine of my life with Sandy and the route. It was a routine that satisfied all of my basic needs and wants, but now this business with Frank had changed my way of seeing things, had given me a sense of possibility I'd never had before. Sandy noticed the difference, I tended to be quieter and to look at things longer. The world had become more mysterious and interesting, and yet more frustrating because I had so little contact with its magic, except through Frank who was deliberately avoiding me.

One day Frank appeared on the dock above us, squinting through his own smoke, smiling. At first, I pretended not to see him, but I knew I couldn't make that little game work. Finally, I looked up at Frank as if I were looking at a stranger.

"Have you got the time of day, sir?"

Frank shook his head and laughed. "Not for the likes of you."

It wasn't easy, but I remained patient and kept loading the car. Sandy just kept on working too. She'd told me that she'd stay out of it unless Frank invited her in, which I was sure would happen sooner or later.

"Have you got a minute?" Frank asked.

I looked at my watch and nodded uncertainly. "Yeah." I handed the keys to Sandy.

Frank met me at his office door and closed it behind us.

"Just wanted to set up an appointment. Tonight, at my place, at seven."

"What if I've already made plans for tonight."

"Don't tell me about it." His dark eyes focused below mine. He smiled. "These chances don't come every day." He picked up a rusty wire cutter on his desk and cut invisible wires. "Will I see you?"

"Probably."

Frank shook his head, tossed the wire cutters on his desk, then spoke very calmly, evenly. "Yes or no, and right now. I don't have time for this shit."

"Alright, I'll be there. But you don't have to be so goddamn stuck up. Why haven't you been talking to me?"

"I never said I was gonna be your buddy. If that's what you're looking for, then you'd better just get out right now while you still can."

"You don't have to be my buddy to be half decent do you?"

"Later. Now get out of here."

I just glared at him for a minute.

"What about Sandy?" I said.

"What about her?"

"Isn't it about time you let her in on this?"

"No."

"What have you got against women?"

"Nothing. But this is between you and me. That's the way it's got to be if it's going to work. Don't bring this subject up again."

On my way out I wanted to slam the door, but managed to control myself. Why did I always have to be mad at Frank? Why did every meeting with him have to be so incomplete and aggravating?

I WAS LIKE a brand new drug addict already broke and needing a fix. I ran up to the door as if I expected it to be locked and barricaded, but it was open, the screen door unlatched, dark inside. I knocked several times, but there was no answer, no sound at all coming from the house.

Suddenly my heart was pounding and I had to breathe deeply several times to calm myself down. I glanced into the front windows, but it was totally dark inside. I felt a tug on my arm and somehow I knew that Frank was waiting for me in the back yard.

I went through a gate at the side of the house and into a fenced-in yard. Frank was sitting in one of two lawn chairs with a small table between them. There were two cans of beer and two glasses already poured.

"Have a seat." Frank grinned, holding up his glass in a toast.

I sat down. "Sorry I'm late."

"No problem." Frank took a long drink.

"Something weird just happened out front."

Frank shook his head. "Don't waste your time thinking about it. You've got to get used to these things and stop walking around with your mouth hanging open. Besides, we have more important things to talk about."

"Yeah, like why you've been giving me the cold shoulder."

"Hell, I wouldn't be talking to you now if I didn't have to."

I stood up. "We can solve that problem real easy."

"Sit down," Frank said.

"I know my way out."

"You mean you're gonna let this garbage get in the way of what you want."

"I can't get it if you don't give it."

"That's exactly right. One of us has got to run this show, and it's got to be me."

I stood there, balling my hands into fists. I'd been doing that ever since I was a little boy, whenever things pissed me off. How often had I actually thrown one of those fists? Never.

"Sit *down*," Frank said, taking out a cigarette.

I sat down. I picked up my glass, but didn't feel like drinking. "I don't like the way this is going." My voice trembled. I hated that about Frank. He always made my voice sound like somebody else's.

"Neither do I," Frank said, taking another drink. "So I guess we're gonna have to set some ground rules."

"Yes sir." I saluted.

Frank glanced at me and shook his head. "First of all you're gonna have to snap out of this sarcastic little boy act."

"Jesus, you're one to talk."

"And you're gonna have to stop trying to hook me into an argument, because I'm not gonna fall for it. I wonder if this kind of behavior has something to do with you running away from home."

It wasn't my voice at all anymore, but it was coming out of my mouth. "It's none of your goddamn business why I left home!"

"Yes it is," Frank said calmly. "From now on everything about you is my business. There's no way we can move from this point if I can't trust you."

"And what if I don't trust *you*?"

"You wouldn't be here if you didn't. You're just mad because you're not in control."

I didn't believe that. In fact I knew he was wrong, and to prove it I kept my mouth shut and stared at the nearest tree. A tall cottonwood.

"Is your head straight enough now for you to listen?"

"Yes," I said, managing to sound almost human.

Frank relaxed into his seat and looked up at the stars. "You've got to understand this business about being hollow." He released a cloud of smoke that drifted away on the cool night air. "As long as you stay all screwed up in these grudges and arguments you don't have a chance. You've got to clear your mind of everything. Then you can give your real attention. You've got to work on this all the time, not just every once in a while. Nothing else can happen, except by accident, until you make some headway on this. Are you listening?"

I nodded.

"Okay. There's another problem. I don't want you to talk to anybody about this but me, and only when I say so. I thought this part was obvious, but I guess I'd better spell everything out to make sure."

"What about Sandy?"

"Let me put it this way. You can't expect to learn anything if every time something happens you go running home to Momma. And I don't expect you to come running home to Daddy either, meaning me. You've got to take what happens to you and hold it inside and see what it turns into."

I stared at my hands, curled together like two dead birds in my lap. "I'm not sure I can handle this."

"When I first started on you, you were real strong. But you've gotten weaker. That happens to some people. So you're gonna have to stay on your toes and work a little harder. Up here." Frank tapped his temple. "You've got to remember yourself. You've got to give up all that hanging on. That's one kind of life. But it's not yours. Not anymore." Frank took another long drag on his cigarette and put it out on the table. "Come on," he said, standing up, "let's go inside."

I FOLLOWED FRANK into the house, which was as dark as a ground hog's hole. All the curtains and shades were drawn, and there were no lights on, no light leaking in. Frank's back almost disappeared in front of me. I bumped into the kitchen table and rebounded into a metal chair. Frank laughed. Down the hall I could barely make out the squares and ovals of pictures on the wall. When we got to the living room, I ran my hand along the backs of the two big familiar chairs and rapped my knuckles against the pole of the reading lamp to help me keep my bearings. Frank sat down in one of the chairs.

"Sit on the couch," he said.

I bumped my shin against the coffee table—which was farther out in the room than I remembered—and worked around to the couch.

"You're not gonna have any skin left on any part of your body," Frank laughed.

"How come no lights?"

"We don't need them."

We sat in silence for a while. I kept expecting Frank to say something, but he didn't. The house was quiet and I was getting real itchy and restless. I squinted into the darkness but couldn't tell if Frank was still there. I knew he had to be there because I would have heard him leave in that silence. I listened for the sound of breathing but couldn't hear it. I started to feel like an idiot and just couldn't stand it any more.

"So what are we supposed to be doing?"

I waited for Frank to answer.

"Frank?" I said. By this time I was beginning to smell a rat.

"Just try to remember yourself and stay alert, as if something was after you," Frank said, breaking that film of silence just when I thought he'd run out on me.

"But what am I looking for?"

"You'll know when you see it. Just be quiet."

I felt a chill run through my body like it did when I was child and my father would scare me. I thought of the watch he gave me tucked away in my drawer, still keeping time. I stayed still for several minutes, waiting. Then I had the strange feeling that something was close to me and I swept my arms through the air, but nothing was there. I started to say something but decided not to. I wanted to pass this test, or whatever it was, without acting like a frightened fool. I tried to relax, sat up straight, and watched and listened as carefully as I could.

But nothing happened. I kept expecting my eyes to grow accustomed to the darkness, but it stayed too thick for me to distinguish anything. All I could see were the swirling fires of my own mind projected on the darkness. Sandy might say that that's all I was ever seeing in those days. Slowly I began to pick up all the sounds around me: small cracking noises in the walls, a car going by, the voices of people in the yard across the street, a dog barking a block away, thumping sounds from the roof as if a cat or squirrel were playing up there, and somewhere, faintly, water dripping in a sink.

I yawned. I found that there were muscles I could use to keep my ears open and more sensitive than usual, but it didn't do much good. I still kept falling half asleep, waking up when my head fell forward. I had no idea how much time had passed. My knee started bouncing up and down in a nervous rhythm and I broke out in a light sweat.

I thought about my route. Tomorrow I would start collecting, which was the only part of my job I didn't like. I especially had trouble with the military people in the trailer parks who sometimes wouldn't pay if I couldn't catch them on pay day. It wasn't one of them that I saw now, but Mrs. Huggins, an old lady who lived in the trailer park. For the last three months she'd managed not to pay me, always saying that I'd caught her at a bad time, and that she would catch up at the first of the month.

I leaned against the three-foot fence that surrounded her small yard and trailer. She was just going in her door with a bag of groceries in her arms. I called out her name and she turned around. She was a small, chunky woman with her white hair pulled up in a bun. She shielded her eyes against the sun with her free hand and smiled.

"Hello young man."

"Mrs. Huggins, I deliver your paper."

"Yes, I know." She swept back a strand of white hair from her forehead.

"Remember? You owe me for the last three months."

"You'll have to come back on the first. That's the only time I have any cash."

"But Mrs. Huggins, this is the second."

"That's right."

"I came by yesterday. I knocked on your door for about fifteen minutes. I could hear the TV and your car was here. I know you were here, Mrs. Huggins."

She smiled coyly and stepped up into the door. "I'm sorry you missed me. You'll have to come back on the first."

She disappeared into the trailer, and I saw the paper I'd thrown earlier still lying on the manicured lawn. I crawled over the fence and looked up to see a large German Shepherd bounding out of the open door of the trailer. It lunged at me but I side-stepped it and hit it on the top of the head with my fist. The dog shook its head and lunged again, getting a mouthful of my shirt as we wrestled each other to the ground. I managed to flip the dog over and grab it by the throat with both hands, the dog digging with all fours at my chest and stomach. I had never felt so enraged, and I strangled the dog with every ounce of my strength until the four legs collapsed beneath me, and the black canine lips flopped loosely over the big incisors. Finally I shoved the dog away. It lay there gasping, the huge pink tongue pulsing on the grass.

I inspected my slashed hands and my shirt which was ripped almost in half. I grabbed the paper and stood up, wiping the dog saliva on my jeans.

"What the hell you doing?" A man with huge arms stood just outside the trailer door. His white T-shirt could not cover all of that hairy beer gut, and his jeans were unzipped.

"I'm taking back my paper," I said. "I paid for it and I'll god-damned if I'm going to give it away."

The man batted his lazy eyelids. He raised his gigantic banana-stalk of a hand to rub his eyes awake. "You ain't goin nowhere with nothin," he said with a slight smile.

"If she wants the paper, she's got to pay for it."

The man looked down at his feet and shook his head, swiped his long blond hair off his forehead. He looked back at me, his eyes squeezed to slits by his prominent forehead and his fat cheeks. "This old woman's got her TV and her newspaper, and that's all she's got, besides me. If that paper stops coming then I'll find you and I'll hurt you real bad."

"I've got to make a living."

"The first thing you got to do is stay alive."

I made a move toward the fence, but the man covered half the yard in one stride. He caught me around the throat with his left hand, lifted me off the ground, ripped the paper from my hand and slapped me across the face with it several times, then threw me bodily over the fence. The man removed the rubber band from the paper and strolled back to the trailer reading the front page. I tried to get up but couldn't move. I felt as though my back was broken and I had no feeling in my legs.

I JERKED AWAKE. That had been the most convincingly real dream I'd ever had. The room was still black and I was sweating. If only Frank would open some windows. My legs really were numb and I changed my position to get my circulation going again. I was feeling more and more stupid by the minute and would have left, but I needed to prove myself to Frank if that was possible, if sitting in a dark room by yourself all night could prove anything.

Again I tried to make myself alert, to make myself watch and listen. But I began to realize I could concentrate for only a few seconds at a time. I couldn't remember myself, understanding for the first time what that meant. I kept thinking of Mrs. Huggins and her knowing smile and the way she always managed to avoid me. I hated to be taken advantage of. Maybe I could get Sandy to go to the door this time and catch her off guard. Maybe I could get Frank to give her a call. I'd like to see that. I'd like to see Mrs. Huggins humiliated into submission. I could just see that antagonistic sweetness of hers melting into defeat.

I shook myself again. My vision of the defeated old woman and her pitiful lawn and my own victorious posture crumbled. Why did I let myself think of myself that way, think of Mrs. Huggins that way? I found again the real world of darkness and silence. But in a moment I saw another image, as if there were a small, automatic projector inside my head.

This time it was a different woman, a beautiful girl whose eyes made me ache inside. She wore a white, clingy cotton dress and she moved before me like a model on a runway, strutting and turning, striking a variety of poses, her eyes never leaving mine for more than an instant. The light behind her brightened and I could see the slender shape of her body through the thin fabric. I didn't recognize her and I didn't know why she was doing this. Finally she stood directly in front of me and began to slowly lift her dress. She smiled, but all I could read in her eyes was curiosity, as if she were studying me, waiting to see what I would do. I pressed the heel of my hand down against my groin. A drop of sweat crawled into my eye. I broke through again to the same old dull silence, her body fading into the chaotic fires of the darkness. I wondered if Frank could see in the dark and could tell what I'd been thinking.

I was exhausted. I just wanted to go home and go to bed and forget all this for a while. I cleared my throat and stretched my legs out in front of me. I finally decided to call it a night no matter what Frank thought of me.

"Frank?" My voice cracked and sounded strange. "Frank, I've had enough of this." But there was no reply.

I waited for a couple of minutes, listening for any movement. I realized that Frank wasn't in the room, that I was alone. I stood up awkwardly, damp jeans sticking to the backs of my legs. I planted my right foot and reached out with my left foot, feeling around, stretching it farther and farther out, but I didn't find anything. Where was the coffee table? I figured I must've shoved it out earlier. I took a short step and again felt around with my foot, but the table wasn't there. I got down on my hands and knees and crawled, extending my right hand out in front of me, but I came to nothing. The two big chairs and the reading lamp were all gone, unless I had just not navigated correctly, but I knew I had. I kept crawling and crawling and reaching out like a blind man, and felt relieved when I finally touched the wall.

I sat there for a minute trying to figure out what the hell could be going on, but couldn't come up with even an unreasonable explanation. I continued to explore the room as best I could. I kept trying to find a light switch, but there didn't seem to be any on the walls, at least not where I thought they should be. I crawled around the room and found it to be completely empty. I couldn't even find the couch I'd been sitting on. Finally I found the window and stood up and pulled back the drapes, but the outside shutters were closed and it was a dark night. A distant street lamp leaked in the slightest bit of light. When I got to the front door I couldn't get it to open, even after I'd made sure it was unlocked. I turned around and yelled out to Frank several times, but there was no answer. My voice echoed in the rooms and halls of the house.

I felt more anger than fear. Frank was making a fool of me. I began to explore the house. All the windows were nailed shut and shuttered from the outside. The side door and back door could not be opened, at least not by me. I ran my hands along every inch of wall that I could reach, but I couldn't find a light switch anywhere.

I paced back and forth in the darkness, finally throwing myself around the room in a rage like the tantrums I used to have when I was a child. My mother's patience had been bewildering. She could always wait me out. When I'd calmed down, I found my way to the kitchen and climbed up on a counter beneath the window. There was a crack in the shutter that allowed me to see a small part of the back yard: the two lawn chairs and the table between, Frank sitting in the chair to the right, one leg draped over the other and a beer in his hand. He took a sip. He seemed to be studying something that was outside my view. I screamed Frank's name as loud as I could, beating on the window, but Frank didn't hear, or was ignoring me.

Then Sandy came into view from the left and sat down in the other chair. They talked. She reached out and put her hand on his forearm. I yelled and banged on the window. Frank shrugged his shoulders and shook his head. They smiled at each other and once Frank let his hand come to rest on her knee for a moment. After ten or fifteen minutes, Sandy left. Frank poured his glass full of beer and settled back down to his meditation.

I wanted to hurt somebody. I could feel my hands around Frank's throat, but I knew I'd never get close enough for that.

I stomped out of the kitchen, lapsing back into my tantrum, cursing Frank for everything I could think of. I kicked the wall and my foot was swallowed up. I yanked my foot out and the wall released a big chunk of plaster and I yelled and danced wildly around the room. I bounced off the wall and tumbled around. I shadow boxed and karate kicked and fell down as if I'd been shot. I kicked another hole in the wall and felt more joy in my heart than I'd felt in a long time. I kicked a hole in the wall of every room. My foot was sore, but it was worth it. If I could have found something else to break, I would've broken it, but there was nothing. I screamed so loud and long my throat ached, but the darkness stayed.

When I grew tired, I leaned against a wall, and my hand went to a light switch. Without thinking I flipped it on and the light surprised me. I stared at the overhead fixture until I felt there was a burning fist in my head, and when I turned away, that huge yellow fist of light blinded me as effectively as the darkness had. In a few seconds my vision began to return. I was in the dining room. It was completely empty. There was not a speck of dust anywhere except where I'd kicked a hole in the wall, and there was plenty of dust there. The kitchen was empty too, except for the built-in counters. Even the electric dishwasher had been removed, leaving a big gap. I went from the kitchen down the hall to the two bedrooms, and both were just as empty and clean.

But the living room wasn't empty. The carpet was still there with the small round impressions where the furniture had been. And the picture of Frank's mother was still on the wall: the dark eyes, the long dark hair, the hand appearing, seemingly out of nowhere, on the table. But there were differences: her look more directly engaging, the barest hint of a smile instead of a broad one. Suddenly I realized that the picture was now only of Frank's mother, his father had disappeared. I studied the picture, noticing every detail: the gold band on the forefinger of that separated hand; the small dark mole on her neck; one very thin, almost invisible braid of hair.

As I turned to leave, I noticed one more thing: in an upper corner of the room, a large spider in her web. I stood beneath her and watched for a moment. I blew against the web and she pulled her legs in, making herself smaller. Suspended in the web near the edge was a bundle wrapped in her silk.

When I got back to the kitchen, the door opened easily, flying away from the slight push I gave it. The light in the kitchen window reached out dimly to where Frank sat, sipping his beer. I strolled out and sat down in the empty chair. All of my anger was gone.

I looked at Frank. He looked back at me, screwed his face up in an amused smile.

"Why don't you rest for a few minutes," he said. "Drink your beer."

The beer was cold. It didn't just taste good, it felt good, a muscular coolness sliding into every part of me. My empty glass dropped to the ground between my feet. I bet I snored.

THE NEXT THING I felt was Frank's hand on my shoulder. The light from the house did not quite touch the upper limbs of the trees swaying in a soft breeze.

I snapped awake and sat up straight in the chair, blinking my eyes.

"You slept without dreaming," Frank said. "You ought to feel better now."

"Jesus, I was out cold. What time is it?"

"I don't know."

"I had some kind of weird dream about your house . . ."

"It wasn't a dream."

"Then what was it? I want to start understanding some of this."

" Basically, it was a lesson in hollowness."

"Frank, let's face it, this hollowness stuff is impossible. For me at least. I am now and forever will be full of shit, and both of us know that."

"That's not quite true. Notice how you're more aware of your own bullshit now. That's a good sign. In fact, you were born with a greater capacity for hollowness than a lot of people. But there's no reason for you to know that. Why do you think I picked you?"

"I don't know, I never really thought about it.

Frank dug into his pocket. He held out a small round stone in the palm of his hand. "Take this home with you. Your goal is to move this stone with that part of you I showed you the first night you came here. Do you remember?"

"I remember. But . . . "

"Don't expect it to happen right away. Put a small piece of paper on top of the stone and try to move it first. That gives you a step in between. Have you got that?"

I nodded. "But what am I supposed to feel? I don't understand how . . . "

"You'll know it when you feel it," he said. "Go home and get some sleep."

I followed Frank into the house. We were through the kitchen and half way down the hall before I realized the furniture was back. Everything was clean and polished. I made Frank wait while I walked all through the house. The holes in the walls had disappeared. I picked up an apple from the center of the dining room table. It was real.

"Take it with you. You look hungry."

"There's one more thing," I said. "I can't believe I almost forgot. What was Sandy doing here?"

"What do you mean?" Frank met my eyes evenly.

"When I was in the house before, I saw Sandy with you in the back yard. What does she have to do with all of this?"

"Sandy has absolutely nothing to do with any of this. And she's never been to this house."

"But I saw her. She sat down in the other chair and touched your arm."

Frank shook his head. "It didn't happen. This is part of the process, Chuck. Your mind is refusing to let go. Just forget it."

I growled in frustration, but Frank took me by the arm, directing me to the front of the house.

When I got to the front door, I looked into the living room. The carpet was gone, leaving a polished wood floor. The picture of Frank's mother was the way I'd first seen it, with Frank's father beside her. And in the far corner the spider and her web with its small bundle were all gone. I turned around and looked at Frank.

"Don't ask." He opened the door.

DRIVING HOME, I tried to figure out what I was doing. But it was clear that I didn't know and couldn't know what I was doing. Hollowness did not sound like such a good idea. What was I supposed to do, scoop myself out like some kind of gourd, and then hang from Frank's clothesline just blowing in the wind? And what could all of that have to do with moving a goddamn stone with . . . with what? my mind? I reached inside my pocket and pulled the stone out, little more than a pebble, but big enough. I felt like I was stuck inside one of those sci-fi novels I'd been getting from the used bookstore around the corner. I'd read enough science fiction to know about psychokinesis. I loved reading about that stuff, but that didn't mean I believed it. My biggest question, though, had to do with Sandy. She lived with me, but I now understood that I didn't know her. Was it even possible to know her? How did she manage to get into this other part of my life that I didn't believe was available to her?

I TOOK OFF my shoes and eased through the door. It was after one o'clock. Street lamps and a bright moon poured light into the room. It was never easy to achieve darkness in these rooms, not that I wanted it dark. I decided not to wake Sandy, and undressed and lay down on the legless couch.

I had a dream, but for once it wasn't about my mother. I guess I should have been relieved. I dreamed I was in the spider's web, but I wasn't afraid. The web was a secret and familiar place, like a child's world beneath tables and behind chairs. The silk package, as large as myself, was suspended on the gently undulating plane of shining threads. The spider was farther off, hanging from beneath the web, as large as a bus, her legs like flying buttresses. She was very still. I wasn't afraid because she communicated to me somehow that she liked me, that she would never hurt me.

I rolled over and the web adapted to me like a hammock. I looked through it into a huge cavern dimly bathed in white light. Everything was vague, great formations of stone and vegetation and maybe of solid wood, though all of this was just guessing. Above me was a wall of whiteness.

Something far away moved. It was another spider, gigantic and muscular, the color of human flesh. Then there was another one, creeping along a stone slab. Suddenly my eyes re-focused, translating everything in a different way. They were hands moving slowly at the same time along the arms of a chair. I found a lap and a chest. Then the head. It was Frank, his head the size of Thomas Jefferson's at Mount Rushmore. When our eyes met, Frank nodded. His eyes dilated, and a thin thread of light slithered out of each one. They traveled across the space and attached themselves to the edge of the web only a few feet from where I lay. The threads swayed and creaked like a rope bridge.

Even then I was questioning everything. I reasoned that nothing that was happening to me could be real. A part of me knew that Sandy was right, that the world did not behave this way. But everything felt so real. Had I been hypnotized, or possessed? Everything felt so real, inside and outside of my dreams. It was all real. And I was myself, the same self I'd always known.

I stayed at this point in the dream for what seemed like many hours. I was still there when Sandy woke me with a kiss.

Chapter Five

SANDY FIXED BREAKFAST and brought it to me on the couch. I drifted in and out of sleep, always returning to the edge of the web, until the smell of hot food woke me for good. I sat up on the couch and ate like a starving man.

"So tell me all about it." She sat on the couch next to me with her own plate of food.

"You mean about last night?"

"What do you think?"

"It was the same old stuff."

"Why were you so late?"

"It wasn't all that late."

"It must have been *pretty* late."

I looked at her, kept on chewing and shrugged my shoulders. "What difference does it make?"

"It doesn't really. I just want to know what you two did. Did he pull any more of his magic stunts?"

"Yeah, a few."

"Like what?"

"Nothing spectacular I guess. He made some things disappear."

"That's interesting. It doesn't sound like his style. What things?"

"Jesus, I don't know. Why this sudden interest in Frank? I thought you didn't like him."

Sandy frowned and stared at me for a minute. "Why aren't you talking to me? You always tell me everything that happens."

"I *am* telling you. Nothing much happened. We drank some beer. He left me alone in the house while something was supposed to happen, he didn't say what, only nothing happened. Then a few things disappeared. It was a waste of time."

"I can tell when you're holding back. You know that."

I dropped the fork in my plate. I knew it was a bit theatrical, but I had to follow through. "I'm not lying."

"You know what I think? I think he's made you promise not to tell me. Jesus, this pisses me off. First you hate him, now you're in love with him. You can't even talk without permission."

"It has to be that way for now." I could hear the melodramatic mysteriousness in my voice, and I hated it.

"This is crazy." She narrowed her eyes, a look she rarely used, almost mean. "I hate all of this," she said in a lower, calmer voice. Then she got up and carried her plate to the sink. Without looking at me she went into the bedroom and closed the door.

I didn't like lying to her, but I felt it was important to do things Frank's way this time, for a change. I took the stone Frank had given me out of my pocket and set it on the table next to my plate. A small gray stone, smooth, almost perfectly round. I made myself keep eating, slowly, casually. Besides, Sandy had been there. She probably knew everything that happened anyway. She might've been testing me to see if I was keeping my word to Frank. I remembered how comfortably they had touched each other, like close friends, or lovers. *She* was the one holding back.

A new trend. Every night Sandy went to bed early to read. This was the first time there had been any trouble between us, and I wasn't crazy about it, but I wasn't about to back off. This is the way I was thinking: Everybody has a right to keep some things to himself. There's no reason why you have to know everything about somebody. There were a lot of things that Sandy hadn't told me, like why she didn't go to see her parents, who lived somewhere in town, and why they never tried to get in touch with her, and why she didn't finish college. It was her business. I didn't have to know.

I figured in a few days we would get back to being friends, and lovers. Maybe we would tell each other more about ourselves. Maybe, in time, I would tell Sandy about my mother.

In those days I rarely let myself think about my mother. It was bad enough that I dreamed about her. I couldn't stop my dreams.

The one good thing about my trouble with Sandy was that it gave me time to practice on Frank's stone. One corner of the living room was my office—a desk and a bookshelf where I did my paper work for the route and kept my collection of fantasy and science fiction novels.

I cleared my desk and set the stone in the middle. I tore off a small piece of paper and balanced it on top. I tried to concentrate, tried to move the piece of paper.

But it was just like it had been at Frank's house, impossible to concentrate for more than a minute at a time. Every sound caught my attention, noises from the hall, from the apartment next door, from the room where Sandy was moving around, from the street. Sometimes I got the feeling that Sandy was watching me and turned around to make sure she wasn't. The thought of her catching me made me . . .

One night Sandy did walk in when I was trying to move the stone. She pulled a chair up beside my desk and sat down. I slid a book over and pretended to be reading.

"Tell me about yourself. About the life you ran away from." Her eyes looked tired. She sat hunched over in her chair, knees together, hands pressed into her lap.

"It was pretty dull, not very much to tell."

She shook her head impatiently. "Chuck, please don't do that to me tonight. We've got to start talking to each other."

I acted like I was in a really good part of my book, but was willing to make the sacrifice for her. I slid a file card in to mark the page and closed the book. "Maybe you're right," I said. I turned my chair around so I could face her. She was wound up tighter than a squirrel on the Fourth of July. So was I. I wanted to reveal something about myself, something that would make her feel we were growing closer.

"I felt I was in the wrong place at the wrong time." I said. "Especially after my mother died."

"What happened to her?"

"Breast cancer. My mother didn't believe in doctors. For everyone else, yes, but not for herself. My father and my brothers and I were always having to go in for checkups she'd arranged, but she never went herself. We got on her case about it, because we thought we could make her feel guilty and then we wouldn't have to go either. And she would promise to go, but she never did. That's the way she was. By the time she noticed something wasn't right and got around to doing something about it, it was too late. She was very strong and she fought it for a long time. The last year of her life was spent mostly in the hospital, a place she hated more than anything."

"I'm sorry Chuck."

"It's okay. It's starting to be a long time ago now."

"What about your father? What's he like?"

"Oh, my father's okay, an interesting man in his own way. His father was a drunk who never could hold a job for very long. My father was always having to quit school and work to help keep the family afloat. Never did finish high school. Had to pass the G.E.D. to get into the Army. He sure did suffer through a lot of bad times with his family. Anyway, when my father was twenty-one he took the whole family to Atlanta and became an auto mechanic. He'd always loved cars and taught himself everything there was to know about them. He spent three years in Viet Nam rebuilding the Army's jeeps and trucks and sent almost every cent he made back to his family. My father's just the opposite of his own dad. When he got back from Nam, he got a job as a car salesman with a big Ford dealership in Columbia, South Carolina. My mother was at the university there and he met her at a party. A year later, after her hopes to make the U.S. diving team had fallen apart, she quit school to marry my father. She was already pregnant with my brother Joe the day they tied the knot. My father was a wiz at selling cars, and after a few years he'd saved enough money to take a chance. He bought into a dealership in Rock Hill and moved us to the home we've had ever since. He turned that business around and made himself into a wealthy man. He still takes care of his mother and father and never has held a grudge against his old man.

"My father worshipped his mother. She was real-deal Christian and so is he. He even became a lay evangelist and started preaching in some of the little churches around Rock Hill. Religion became the only real source of conflict between my mother and father. My mother always did her own thinking about things and my father could never turn her into the dedicated Christian he wanted her to be.

"I think the maddest I ever saw my father was on those Sunday mornings my mother decided to sleep in. She just wouldn't go to church unless she felt like it, and sometimes she didn't feel like it. She'd be lying there with the pillows piled up on her head and my father would be standing beside her dressed up like the big shot preachers he'd seen in Atlanta and Charlotte, and he'd be spouting every bit of Christian trickery he could think of, all designed to make her feel guilty so she'd do what he wanted her to. He'd say that Eve was made from the rib of Adam and that a woman was supposed to follow the direction of her husband. He'd say she was setting a bad example for her children, especially me since I hadn't been officially saved. A lot of times he'd tell how embarrassing it was for him when people at church asked about her and he would find himself lying and telling them she wasn't feeling well. Sometimes I'd get mad at her too because I had to go to Sunday School and church with my father whether I felt like it or not, and it didn't seem fair that she could stay all snuggled up in bed while I had to dress up in uncomfortable clothes and be quiet and polite for three hours while a bunch of grown-ups told me a lot of things about Jesus I never could make sense of. I mean, why would God allow his Son to be tortured to death, even for a worthy cause? It seemed to me that God could solve the world's problems any way he wanted to. Only a cruel or stupid God would resort to all this crucifixion business.

"Anyway, my mother was never really persuaded, and my father just had to learn to put up with her. Even when she did go to church with him, she was a problem. She wore these knockout dresses that showed off her figure, and she had a beautiful body. He was a nervous man when he was with her in public, always afraid he was going to have to defend her honor. One time at a football game some fellow made a suggestive remark to Mother as he passed by, and my father didn't take any time for talking or threats or anything like that. He just went over and hit the man one time and the man went down and that was the end of it. The other time I heard about happened at a movie. A man said something about my mother to a friend of his, but he said it out loud so everybody could hear. My father jumped right on him, but this man was used to getting into fights and he was ready. They knocked each other all over that lobby for about ten minutes before a cop broke it up. The man that was telling the story said that there was blood all over the carpet and walls. He said that getting my father off that man was like trying to pull a Pit Bull off a mailman. My father wasn't normally violent, being a Christian and all, but when it came to my mother he had a really short fuse, and everybody knew it. After that fight in the theater, men tended to be real respectful toward my mother. Considering all the trouble she caused my father, I think he would've left her if he hadn't been so crazy about her. She was his one great weakness and he knew it and he prayed for her soul every day. And his own soul too, because he could never keep his hands off her for five minutes.

"That's why it damn near killed him when she got sick and he knew she was going to die. He felt like the Lord was punishing both of them, her for resisting the call of Christ, and him for loving her more than he loved God. After she got sick, he was very devoted to her. He never stopped trying to save her soul, but he was so good to her that she put up with it. She talked to me about my father because she knew we had similar feelings toward him, and she knew she could trust me. She said that for his sake she'd considered giving in to him and accepting Jesus as her Savior, but she could never do it, partly because she just didn't believe it, and partly because she wanted him to see that God was not small, that God didn't need Jesus in order to love His people just as they were. But of course my father could never see things that way. My mother died an agnostic, and my father managed to convince himself that she had come to Jesus in her own way before she died. But I knew better. I knew it for certain."

Sandy reached out and put her hand on mine, and I knew that I'd done the right thing, telling her all of this. "What makes you so sure?" she asked.

"I was the only one with her when she died." I paused, looked directly into her eyes. "And I know that Jesus was the farthest thing from her mind."

After that, I wouldn't answer any more questions. She was good about it. She let it drop.

SHE FOLDED PAPERS and dropped them over her shoulder into the back seat. Everything about her was beautiful. The way her eyes lifted from her hands and found the afternoon sun low on the rooftops. Her mouth had these clean little lines, like parentheses, around the corners. Her hands were graceful and strong folding the papers. I didn't want to lose her, but I knew I had to confront her, and that wasn't going to be easy.

"I guess I need to talk to you," I said.

"You guess?"

"The problem is . . . I know what's bothering you but you don't know what's bothering me."

"Okay. I'm listening."

I pulled the car over, turned off the engine and stared into the plastic web of the steering wheel.

"Well, are we just going to sit here?" she said, throwing another paper over her shoulder.

I turned in the seat and faced her. "Do you promise to tell the truth?"

"Jesus," she said, rolling her eyes. "Okay, cross my heart and hope to die." She crossed her heart. "Satisfied?"

"Why the sarcasm?"

"You don't trust me to tell you the truth?"

"Of course I trust you."

"Then why do you ask me to promise?"

"You're right. I'm sorry."

"What did you want to ask me?"

I took a deep breath. This was it. I really wasn't sure that she would tell me the truth. "What were you doing over there?"

I watched her face carefully. She blinked her eyes, slowly shook her head. "What are you talking about?"

"Sandy, I'm getting so tired of this game."

"Then stop playing it," she said, raising one eyebrow.

"I just can't trust you anymore."

"Shit," she said. She searched for words for a moment, and when she spoke, turning to me, she emphasized each word slowly. "I . . . haven't . . . done . . . anything . . . wrong. You're the one acting weird."

"So you deny it."

"Deny what?"

"That you were over there goddamnit! Because if that's what you're saying then you're the one that's lying, and I can't handle that from you."

"You're talking about Frank aren't you?"

"What the hell else would I be talking about?"

"Anything would be fucking great. He's making you crazy."

"And what's he making you?"

She screwed up her face. "What does that mean? I don't even know the man, and don't *want* to know him. He's just a half-dead looking creep at the newspaper building as far as I'm concerned."

"He's more alive than anybody I've ever known."

Sandy looked away from me and shook her head. "One minute you despise him, the next minute you love him. I wish you'd make up your mind and do what you have to do."

"Okay, I admit I'm confused."

"It's worse than that. You're letting him screw us up. He's been trying to get rid of me ever since I first showed up, and he's finally found a way to do it. The two of you are such a goddamn exclusive little club. You know that?"

"You still haven't answered my question."

"I've never been to Frank's house if that's what you mean. I've never even seen the place."

"So you deny it?"

She looked at me amazed. "Of course I deny it! Why would I go to his house?"

"Looking for me maybe. Or maybe you're in with him."

"What does that mean? . . . in with him. Why would anybody want to be in with him?"

"This isn't working out, is it?"

"You've got to do your part. He's made you promise not to talk to me, hasn't he? That's what's getting in the way."

"Yeah, I promised. There are reasons. But it doesn't really matter, I wish you could believe that. If I told you what happened that night, you'd laugh, just like the other times. You'd start talking about mirrors and trick photography or something. Besides I've already told you the most important thing that happened, which was seeing you. That's the thing that's driving me crazy, you were there and you won't explain, you just keep pretending like you don't know what I'm talking about."

"I don't know what you're talking about. If I did know, like you claim, then what harm could there be in telling me what I already know? You're so confused you're making me confused. What it boils down to is that you don't trust me enough to talk to me and you don't believe what I say. Look at me, look at my eyes." She took my face in her hands. "Do I look like I'm lying to you? I don't have anything to do with Frank, and I've never been to his house. Okay? But you still don't believe me, do you?"

"I don't know. It's hard not to believe what you see."

"When you're with him, everything you see is *him*, or his doing, haven't you figured that out by now? He's a magician, he creates illusions."

"He's a lot more than that."

"The problem is you've bought his whole routine and you idolize him, you know, like a hero. He's more than an ordinary human to you."

"Well, he *is* more than ordinary."

"I'm sure it would please him to hear you say that."

"No. Just the opposite."

"Right, he's not an ordinary man, he's humble, he's perfect. And you want to be more than ordinary too. And so you believe everything he says and does. You want what you think he has, only he won't give it to you and it's driving you crazy. He's got you by the balls and there's nothing you can do about it except just get out of it, only you want it too bad to do that."

"We're not getting anywhere with this."

"No, we're not. All I know is, it's hard for me to live with a man who doesn't trust me."

"Are you threatening me?"

She leaned toward me and put her hand on my thigh. It was all I could do to keep from flinching.

"No. It's not a threat. I'm just telling you the truth, that's all. I will not live with a man who doesn't believe what I say."

I shook my head, turned away from her and stared out at the passing cars. There was nothing I hated more than deception, and I hated how effective at it she'd become. I came so close to believing her. But what would that mean? That I hadn't seen what I knew that I had seen. I'd never been so frustrated, so angry, in my life, and I had no way to express this anger. She knew how important she was to me. The implied ultimatum she'd given me made me even madder.

I started the car and with a glance at oncoming traffic pulled out in front of a truck . . . the hiss of air brakes, squeal of tires. I slowed down to a taunting crawl. The truck driver pounded on his horn and yelled obscenities out his window. Sandy just stared at me.

EVERY NIGHT FOR many years I had dreamed about my mother, returning to her hospital room on the night she died. Now I had this new dream that took its place. It wasn't frightening. I always felt safe and relaxed. Everything moved slowly and was out of focus, too close or too far away. The silk package always floated nearby, mysterious as an averted face. And the spider herself was a dark cloud hovering beneath the web a short distance away until I held my eyes on her. She always faced me. Her legs arched miraculously into the distance away from the huge, dark bulk of her body, the oblong bubbles of her eyes black and shiny like sun-glasses, her black jaws, sometimes moving slightly, gateposts into a dark cave. Still, as ominous and powerful as her form was, I never feared her. I knew she could have killed me long ago if that was what she wanted. The vibrations I felt along the threads were welcoming, protective even. The dream always ended with me at the web's edge, two threads drifting down into vast space where they finally connected to the chair in which Frank sat waiting. They swayed in the wind and made little popping sounds like clothes hung out to dry.

ONE AFTERNOON SANDY didn't feel like going with me on the route. When I returned, she was gone, along with her clothes and other things. I found a note pinned to a pillow on the bed:

Dear Chuck,

I love you. I wish I could make you believe that I had nothing to do with Frank. But I know I'll never be able to convince you since you won't even believe Frank. For you, what you see is what you know. For me, life plays too many tricks to ever be sure of anything. Maybe that's the scientist in me, the skeptic. Sometimes I fantasize that I could prove to you that Frank's magic is no more real than a dream. But then I remember something that I've known for a long time, that we believe what we want to believe, need to believe. I think deep down you know this too, but I can't seem to reach that place in you.

What we had at first was great. I really don't care anything about money or having a lot of things. I could have lived like that forever. But you've changed. I've been around enough relationships gone sour to know I don't want one of my own. I'd rather have it end right here while there's still more of the good part to remember than the bad.

I'm not going far away. You could find me if you want to but please don't. I want to be alone for a while and then I want to start my life over. I feel like I'm nowhere. I've got to figure out what I want to do and what I want to be. Besides, the coldness I feel in you is not going to go away. You've got things to do, with Frank and all of that, and I'm in the way.

Please don't forget that I love you.
Sandy

I lay on the bed and read the note over and over. What a fool I was. I hadn't really expected her to leave. I thought I'd be able to figure out what she was doing at Frank's and it would be something we could work out together. Maybe she'd promised Frank not to tell and she was just better at keeping the promise than I'd been. It could be another one of Frank's tests. She'd kept her secret while I'd let suspicion get the best of me.

She was right about one thing: Frank had sure found a way to come between us. It had only been a few hours since I'd seen her and already I was hurting. I figured this must be like the withdrawal pain that addicts feel, but I didn't like thinking of her as only a drug that I had to have. For the first time I realized how attached to her I was. Still, I would honor her wishes. Her note said that Frank wanted her out of the way. I believed that part of it was true.

Chapter Six

I LET MY eyes drift back to that small slip of paper on top of the round stone, resting in the spot of light from my reading lamp. The darkness in my window darkened. I could feel the world outside pulling towards me as if I were a vacuum, but I still couldn't move the slip of paper. It didn't bother me though. I'd been trying to do this for over a year, and I no longer expected the paper to move. I just liked the way trying to move it made me feel, as if I were the eye of a storm.

I hadn't spoken to Sandy since the day she left. The pain of her absence was a constant, but I put it in the background and kept going. It was something I'd always been able to do. Some part of me walked away from her just as I'd walked away from my home in South Carolina, from my father and brothers, from the pain of my mother's death. Was this what Frank had seen in me, this ability to step clear of things? Was this what he meant by hollowness?

I had seen Sandy a few times on the street, and when our eyes met all the old feelings came back. But I made no effort to talk to her, mainly because nothing had changed. I was still running the route, but Frank had practically no contact with me. I knew no more about Frank's powers than I'd known a year ago. For a long time I'd done everything I could to get Frank to talk to me, to show me more, but he would have no part of it. He acted like nothing had happened. After so long I was beginning to wonder if anything had.

Frank had added on to my route, and I had over 500 customers now. It took me nearly four hours to make the complete run. I'd also signed on as a substitute driver for the weekend truck routes. In a good month I could make seven or eight hundred dollars, but I had little use for it. I spent most of my spare time walking or drinking beer or sitting in my room trying to make one small piece of paper move. I didn't have the slightest feeling for this blob of light inside myself that I must somehow find and activate and train like a good dog.

Nothing made me so aware of the fact that I was getting nowhere as the dream. It was there every night, and it was always the same.

Sometimes in the morning or early evening I would go for a long walk in the city. I especially liked the old part of town, the carefully maintained buildings with gargoyles and statues of voluptuous winged maidens presenting scrolls. Hovering over this old heart of the town were newer glass skyscrapers whose lights burned all night, and gigantic hotel convention centers with glass elevators and botanical gardens. To the west the Rocky Mountains crouched over the city. There were numerous parks with cement walks wandering among dark, old trees and iron benches. Colorado Springs had its share of crime, but the streets were basically busy and safe. It was a city of cool summers and cold winters, but the winter air was dry and the snow itself was dry and inviting. I liked to walk around looking at the people, sometimes stopping to speak with someone. I liked to browse in old book stores and pawn shops, but almost never bought anything. In the thoughtful moods that grew out of my concentrated solitude, I was looking into the eyes of this city for the first time.

There was a bar and grill down the street from my apartment called The Sha Na Na where I liked to go at night to have a couple of beers and eat and listen to the jukebox. In the late mornings I sometimes went to an old restaurant called The Elite where I would take a table near the window, drink iced tea and eat a sandwich if I was hungry.

One fall day I was sitting at my usual place by the window drinking my tea and looking out at the street. The restaurant was practically empty. I had brought a copy of yesterday's *Sun* with me, but it was still rolled up on the table in front of me. All I could do on this day was think about my life of running away that had brought me to this point. I was twenty-one years old. I had almost no education, no talent that I knew of, no close friends, no family, no lover, no plans. I felt that I'd been suspended from ordinary life. If there was a war I supposed I would go, but there wasn't even that.

The restaurant began to get crowded, and I realized I'd stayed too long, into the early lunch hour. I stood to go, but I noticed a woman sitting alone at a booth. She looked up at me and I felt the pressure of her eyes against me and noticed the long dark braid of her hair. She made no gesture of invitation, but I walked over to her booth anyway and stood there silently for a moment while she studied me.

"Sit down," she said, finally.

It had never occurred to me before that a woman well into her sixties, or was it her seventies?, could be beautiful, but she was beautiful. Her hair was as gray as it was black, parted in the middle and pulled back on each side into the strands of her long braid. Her eyes had the soft gray luminescence of an overcast sky. She had the high cheekbones of an Indian and the dark brown skin of a Gypsy. Her hands were long and muscular with short, clear fingernails. There was a slightly unkempt air about her, a few hairs pulled loose and flying around her otherwise sleek head, and wrinkles in her plain, dark blue dress. She took a few bites of food during our conversation, but I could tell that eating didn't interest her. She was as slender as a sanderling.

The booth—with the wall on one side and the tall dark backs of the benches on two other sides—held a privacy, a quietness, I'd never noticed before.

"Do you know who I am?"

I nodded. "Yeah, you're Frank's mother."

She smiled. "And you're the young man I've heard so much about."

"From Frank."

She cocked her head, but in a smooth, sliding motion. "He thinks an awful lot of you."

"He's never given *me* that feeling."

"Well, he's not one to show it in the usual ways."

"How did this meeting happen? Have you been following me?"

"No," she said, laughing. "There's no need to follow you. You're easy to find. I would have come to your apartment, but Frank says I would have no place to sit. I can't go back to sitting on the floor at my age."

I shook my head and laughed. "Frank hasn't been to my place in years. What would he know? I have a place for you to sit."

"It doesn't matter. We're here now aren't we?"

"Yes."

"Now. What shall we talk about?"

I shrugged. "I don't know. I feel like I've been in the dark so long, and now I can't think of anything."

She smiled.

"I know. What about your husband, Frank's father, is he still alive?"

"Oh, no, he's been dead for years. Fifteen years older than me you know. A beautiful man. A great man, and few people realized it, except those of us who knew him well. The kind of man that gave everything and took little. If he had any weakness, it was that he took nothing. Frank is that way. Very much like his father. You may not see it yet, but it's true. It's at no small cost to himself that he's given so much to you."

"I don't follow that." I brandished my rolled-up *Sun*. "This is all I get from Frank. Five hundred of 'em every day."

"He's never liked displays of light and power. Thinks they're vulgar I suppose, cheap. Gives a demonstration only when he has to, to wake somebody up."

"Okay. What about this? Are we really all connected together with these threads of light?"

"Oh, my goodness yes." She gazed into the crowded room. "You mean you can't see it?"

I didn't know what to say.

"My dear boy, you are missing a beautiful sight. In a room full of people like this, it's quite dazzling."

I looked into the room. All I could see was the people themselves, talking, eating, looking for a table.

"Well don't worry about it," she said. "Your time will come. That's what Frank is doing you know, trying to scoop out a little space in you. Even some scientists, bless their hearts, are starting to see the connection. We are all made of light, just bursting with it. I read about these things in the magazines." She leaned towards me, reached out and patted my hand. She gazed directly at me, an immense reservoir of strength behind those dusky eyes. Her hand rested on mine, the first time in a while I could remember someone touching me. I suddenly felt nervous.

"Why are we having this conversation?" I asked.

"I thought it might be a good idea."

"Did Frank put you up to this?"

"Of course not. What a silly question."

"Does he know you're here?"

She cocked her head again, slow-motion, but still bird-like. "Oh dear, you ask all the wrong questions. A chip the size of Pike's Peak on your shoulder."

"Why don't you knock it off," I blurted before I could stop myself.

Her hand moved away from mine. "Oh, it gets worse. The taunting of a small boy."

I ignored her. "Maybe this whole thing was just a trick, like Sandy said."

"Yes. It's just a trick." She looked down at the table. The knife next to her plate, flecked with bits of food, slid across the table toward me. I slapped it with my newspaper and held it down.

"Watch it!" I said.

"It's you who'd better watch it," she said, laughing.

Suddenly the knife came alive under my paper, and I had to grab it by the handle with both hands. I could feel that strange pulling in my stomach. The knife angled toward me and I tried to hold it away, but it hovered in my double fist a foot away from my chest.

"I could make it look like suicide." Her eyebrows pulled together, making a sharp furrow above her nose. "I can see the headlines: 'Young Man Stabs Self To Death In Restaurant.'"

The knife moved till the tip of the blade pressed against my sternum. I pulled against it as hard as I could, my arms shaking. I glanced around, but no one had noticed what was happening.

"Now tell me this is a trick," she said calmly. I could have panicked, but I didn't. Some sort of space opened in me, and I knew that she wouldn't hurt me right there in that restaurant. I took my hands off the handle and the knife remained suspended against my chest. Still no one else appeared to notice. When I met her eyes, they stunned me, like nothing I'd ever seen. Black water, glinting. But bottomless, like one of those lakes in a cave. The knife trembled against me like the quill of a feather. Then it fell into my lap.

I grabbed it, slapped it back on the table. "You wouldn't have done it."

"Of course I wouldn't. But you don't understand that, do you?"

"Too many people around."

"People or no people. I wouldn't hurt you, or anyone else." She brought her napkin to her mouth for a moment, then placed it back on the table. "We've talked too much, I think." She shook her head very slowly. "Too many words aren't good for you. Like candy, you know. Make you feel good or bad for a while, but no substance. Especially bad for a child."

I wanted to say something defiant, like always, but I felt she was so far over my head that I would drown in her if I even breathed.

She studied me, like one of those bugmasters over the carcass of a beetle, turning her head into various positions, her eyes moving over me. "It's true," she said, talking to herself in an analytical tone, "there is a certain excavated space in you." She reached across the table and touched me above the heart with her index finger. "But landlocked." She made a circle on my chest around the original point. "That which remains is strong, maybe the wrong kind of strength." She removed her finger and sat back. "But, it's not my decision. I thought there

was something I could say that would help you, but apparently not."
Then she got up from her seat.

"Wait a minute. There's got to be more to it than that?"

"Even Frank can get impatient," she said. "Take action, or it will
be too late."

"But he won't have anything to do with me."

"Maybe it's all for the best. You're not ready to be one of us."

She turned to go but I reached out and caught her wrist. "But
what about my dream? What does it mean?"

"Ah yes, your dream. But there's no time now."

"And what about Sandy? I need to know where she fits in."

"You mean that little tart you used to sleep with?"

I tightened my grip on her arm. "*Don't* you . . ."

"I thought that might get a rise out of you." She pulled her wrist
out of my hand. "You're a very predictable boy. Pushbutton. Good
luck." She walked away and out the door without paying.

I stayed at the booth for a few minutes trying to calm down.
What kind of action was she talking about?

Then suddenly I was ashamed. And angry. I had just been in the
presence of the most exceptional human being I would ever know,
and all I could do was act like the spoiled, greedy child that I was.

I sat there for another ten minutes with the lunch crowd gathering around me. Who was to blame for my dead-end situation? I
knew it was me. For the first time, I knew it. I could not blame my
mother or my father or my brothers. I had just demonstrated to
myself the self that kept me down. Maybe the seed of it was in being
the kid brother who had to act tougher than he was to keep up with
his older brothers. Maybe the flowering of it was in those years on
the road alone, a kid having to act like a man to get a job, even the
worst sort of job. That wasn't it. I could feel a lot more underneath
the words, clinging to my bones. More than just the stereotypical
explanation. Except that part about acting like something I wasn't.
I was a pretender alright, even to myself.

THE SUN'S BACK lot was deserted when I pulled in. Frank strolled out and stood on the edge of the dock, cigarette dangling from his mouth. He nodded toward a stack of bundles.

"Phieffer kept an eye on them for you."

"Would you thank him?"

Frank nodded.

"Sorry I'm late."

Frank just stared and rocked back and forth in that familiar square stance of his.

"I have a good excuse," I said. "I was talking with your mother."

The flicker of a smile, a glimmer of light in Frank's eyes.

"She said I should come to see you, said I should do it soon."

The smile turned into smoke, the light faded.

"Hey Frank. Why don't you ride with me today? I sure could use the help."

"Got my own work to do."

I manufactured my best grimace, shook my head. "If I leave this thing up to you, Frank, I'll never get any farther."

Frank nodded. "That's right." He turned and walked back toward his office.

"Damnit Frank, I don't know what to do anymore!"

Frank stopped at his door and looked back at me. "Then don't do anything. And don't talk about it around here, or anywhere else either. Don't you have any sense?" He closed the door behind him.

I started throwing bundles into my back seat. Frank was a weird, sad character, I thought. A dark little man with secret powers he didn't use. He could have anything he wanted. Instead, he held on to a basically menial job and lived alone in a shabby little house. I was beginning to wonder why I'd stayed with this thing for so long. Was I going to end up being a strange little man like Frank? Is that the way I already was? I decided the answer was "no." I would use my powers more intelligently if I ever managed to get them.

I parked out on the street and mechanically rolled my papers, thanking God there were no inserts today. On the route some of my customers, especially the older ones, were waiting for me on their porches or in the front yard. A couple of them were looking under bushes and cars. I apologized to them as best I could. Even under these circumstances, it was a relief to talk in a plain way to ordinary people.

I JUST WANTED to go back to the beginning of this whole mess and make some different decisions, establish some fairer terms for myself.

At night especially I could not escape my growing sense of frustration. My apartment, which I'd been cleaning and ordering religiously for the last year, returned to chaos, with clothes and books everywhere and dirt and trash piling up, spider webs claiming every corner. I gave up on my concentration exercises, though the rock and small slip of paper remained solemnly unmoved in their small shrine on my desk. In my restless frame of mind there was nothing in particular I wanted to do and no place I wanted to go. It made me feel sick to realize that the only two people I really wanted to see would have nothing to do with me. I had some friends that worked at *The Sun*, but the idea of sitting through hours of their small talk about football and local politics was almost nauseating. I felt my whole life had become a disease.

I would have bought a bottle of whiskey, but drinking in large amounts just knocked me out, and made me jumpy and exhausted the next day. These inconveniences wouldn't bother me if the booze could somehow release me from my problems, but I knew it couldn't. It used to be that alcohol obliterated my mind and sent me into a peaceful, dreamless sleep. But not any more. When I passed out on the couch or bed, at first I would be spinning and falling and then suddenly I was caught by that same web of the dream. The silence was a painful fullness in my ears. Moving at all was a drudgery. And always there was the spider, the white package, the precipice edge of the web, the two fine ropes flying off into space to the chair where Frank came slowly into focus, his two hands like grotesque spiders themselves crawling on the arms.

One night when I awoke sweaty and sick from my dream, the first thing my eyes opened on was a spider in her empty web in the corner above me. There was one long thread bowing in the soft air from a vent, a sliding needle of light anchored to the arm of the couch next to my head. I jumped up, scrambled to my closet, grabbed an old broom and raked the web down. The spider clung to the broom and charged up the handle toward my hand. I threw the broom down and chased the spider under several pieces of furniture. I finally corralled her in a corner and killed her with a shoe. It was a common house spider. The same kind that had been in Frank's house, the same kind that lived in my dream. This fact did nothing to calm me down. She'd been working inches from my face to attach that strand. Were the spiders in league with Frank too?

I put on some clothes and went out, found an all night bar, a dark corner away from the second-shifters raising hell, and drank until morning. Then I called *The Sun* and they connected me with Frank. I said I was sick and Frank said okay and that was that.

I laughed into my drink. There was no one but myself who knew the route well enough to drive it efficiently. When Frank added to the route, it was me who explored the territory, carefully mapping the most efficient pattern, getting permission to use certain back alleys and driveways. It was the only thing in my life I'd created on my own, and I'd been hesitant to teach it to the subs that Frank kept on call. It did me good to think of Frank slowly hassling his way through the cranky maze of that route with nothing but a rough list of names and addresses to go on.

I drove straight home and went to bed, wrapping myself in the sheets so that there was only a small hole for air near my face. And for hours it seemed, and for the first time in weeks, I slept soundly.

And when I did dream, it wasn't about the spider. Not at first. It was Frank driving the route. Papers leaped wildly out of the car, diving into chimneys, landing in barbecue grills, slapping small children to the ground, flying up ladies' dresses causing them to scream and run amuck. One paper flapped open like two bodiless wings into the face of an old man who wrestled it to the ground. Hundreds of them flopped into birdbaths and mud-holes and the slobbering mouths of dogs. Frank laughed so hard he could barely raise his arm to throw the papers, which jumped out of his hand like lunatic birds. He drove through stop signs, red lights and the wrong way up one-way streets as cars dodged him crashing among screams and the sounding of horns. Somewhere a phone kept ringing and Frank's laughter turned to weeping.

Suddenly there was silence, the steady throbbing of wind, the slowly rocking strands of the web. And I was scared this time. Just plain scared.

THIS TIME WHEN I came to the edge, I remembered something: a voice, the vague shape of an amused face, Frank's mother leaning across that table speaking in a low voice much like the tone one would use to coax a child into doing something it wanted to do anyway, the way my mother used to summon me into the cold water of the lake. "Take action," the old woman had said. *This*, I knew, was what she meant, these white strands extending like the last ropes of hope in an adventure film down into this great cavern of a room. Why hadn't I seen before how obvious an invitation this was? I felt crazy. It was only a dream and I could not die in a dream and there was no real pain that could reach me in a dream. I could do anything I wanted.

I sighted down the strands and they bowed and swayed in the air currents, but they seemed taut enough to hold me steady. I reached out with my right hand and took a secure grip on one of the strands, which had about a one-inch diameter with the weight of a sturdy cord. Like the web itself, it was almost sticky, though it left no residue on the skin. The angle was steep, but I knew I wasn't going to be able to slide down these cords, not with my bare hands. It would be hand over hand all the way. Slowly I brought my left hand out to the other cord and let my body fall free from the web, dangling now in the open.

I immediately felt a heavy trembling of the web carried down into the cords. Looking over my left shoulder, I saw her coming, a huge black engine gliding upside down under the web, damp and gleaming. I hand-walked down the cords as far as I could, thinking if she started after me I was going to put an end to this dream. But she didn't. She stopped at the edge of the web and reached down with one claw, slightly crimping a cord. Suddenly it went slack and I let it go and hung now by both hands to the remaining cord. The loose strand rippled and curled in the space beneath me, finally drifting out of sight. I just held on for a minute, waiting to see if she would cut the other cord, but she didn't.

I started working my way down again, hand over hand, trying to assess the distances, the space. If I were to let go now it would be like dropping from a plane into the Grand Canyon. Beneath me in the distance there were huge rock-like platforms and cliffs which I knew must be the furniture in Frank's living room. The further on the line I went, the more impossible I felt my situation to be, but I had no place else to go and nothing better to do. I just kept putting one hand in front of the other.

As I moved away from the web, there were many objects floating in the air around me, attaching to my body like velcro or lashing across my face. I figured they must be larger particles of dust, so light they were little more than an aggravation. They were of every conceivable shape and color, giving a kind of substance to the air, a loose jumble of tumbling debris.

But then I became aware of something that might be more of a problem. At first it was a fast-fluttering sound, almost like a car engine with a knock. When something large and gray flashed in front of me, my stomach turned over and I decided I wanted out of this dream now. I kept telling myself, "Wake up! Wake up!" but I didn't wake up. My hands were aching so badly they were almost numb, but I just kept moving them. Then it came back, hovering in front of me, the heavy but fast pulsing of those wings throbbing in my head. It was about twice my size. It darted around me, sometimes stopping in mid-air to study me. I studied back. The lower bulb of its body was a dirty-white on the bottom with a line of black hair through the middle to the pointed tip at the end. The upper part of the body sprouted six legs that were folded away in flight. Its back was striped, that dirty white alternating with a dark gray and all of it sparsely swept with stiff black hair. Its veined wings were translucent and almost invisible while in motion, which created the illusion that the creature moved through space only by an act of will, giving it a frightening kind of freedom. But what fascinated me the most as I kept working my way down the cord was the creature's huge, mobile head. There was a red, round button the size of a hubcap on each side with thousands of lenses, each reflecting a sharp image of my body, which I realized for the first time was entirely naked. From the lower middle part of the creature's head, the slight movements of a long black proboscis. In short bursts, I caught the foreign stench of its breath.

At first I kicked out and it moved away, but I could sense that it had no fear of me and that I was vulnerable to any assault. Each time I kicked out, the strain on my hands and the drain on my energy forced me to stop and regroup. Finally, I was just hanging there with the beast flying around me in smaller and smaller circles. I closed my eyes. I began to think the best thing I could do would be to let go. Then this dream could come to the end that all of my falling dreams had come to. I would jump up in the bed with a groan and that would be it. But I didn't let go. I hung there with my eyes closed and the roar of wings in my ears, drifting into what was almost a second level of sleep within the dream.

Then the creature was on me, the four lower legs stabbing my sides and thighs, something rough and wet like the giant tongue of a cat covering my face. A shudder went through my body. Somehow my hands didn't give way with the added weight. They wouldn't last much longer. But they didn't have to. I felt the tension in the cord snap from the upper end and the creature separated from me. I was falling, but I had the weight of an ant and it was more like drifting downward, slowly sinking into a world that towered above me. I landed in the soft, thick fibers of the carpet with a jolt, but I wasn't hurt. I got to my feet as soon as I could, envisioning mortal combat with a giant roach. But a hand the size of a great tree was descending from the sky and landed palm upward beside me. It was a damp world of shallow swirling trenches and gullies, a great open-air elevator. I was just tall enough to scramble aboard and was lifted up beside a huge flowing surface of changing colors and textures that I knew must be Frank. I heard a tremendous eruption of sound that I thought was monumental laughter. It would have been frightening in itself, but nothing could frighten me now. Another hand appeared above me like a thundercloud, and then there was darkness and silence.

I EMERGED FROM a great white cloud of silence. When I finally moved, the sheets were cool and my body was comfortable, lazy. I was too weak to make a good fist.

My bedroom door was closed. Who had closed it, and why?

I sat up, suddenly remembering my dreams. The first one, about Frank running my route, seemed to have no meaning. I let it go. But the spider dream had taken a new direction, and I remembered everything about it. My body was aching, exhausted, and I couldn't believe it was possible to feel such hunger.

There were footsteps outside my door. The doorknob turned and I slid back under the sheets and pulled them up to my neck. Frank's head popped in, big grin on his face.

"You're awake," he said and swung the door wide. I felt the presence of others behind him in the outer room, but I could see no one.

"I'm not so sure. How did you get in here?"

"No such thing as a locked door, not for me." He sat on the edge of my bed and pulled out a pack of cigarettes from the inside pocket of his jacket. He'd changed somehow, something different in his eyes.

"Okay," I said. "Then *why* are you here?"

"Do you remember your dreams?" His left hand slid down the length of my shin and encircled my ankle through the sheet. It was a strange sensation and I stiffened and wanted to pull my leg away, but I made myself breathe deeply, relax and be still.

"Yeah, as a matter of fact I do."

"Tell me about them." He gently stroked my ankle. It felt really good, better, I realized, than anything I'd felt in a long time. Goosebumps ran over my body. A deep breath possessed me.

I looked out the window, calling the dreams' vivid scenes back to my mind, gazing at the late morning sun ascending the rough old face of the building across the street. "I dreamed about you at first. You'd taken my route." I laughed. "You went berserk, making the papers do all kinds of crazy things to people."

"Okay." Frank matter-of-factly blew smoke out the side of his mouth. "Now tell me about the other one."

"Yeah. It was even weirder. More like a nightmare. It started out the same as always. I've been having this same dream for over a year. I've been trying to tell you about it, but you never would let me."

"Well, I'm listening now."

As I told him about the dream, Frank nodded often, encouraging me to recall every detail.

"It was a long fall," I said, "but I was as light as a corn flake and didn't get hurt. Then this giant hand picked me up. I assumed it was your hand. Then you closed your other hand over me, it got dark, and that was the end. Except for the laughing. I heard you laughing, I think."

"It was a big step for you Chuck. And a big relief for me."

"You make it sound like you were there."

"I *was* there. You saw me."

"Yeah, but Frank, it was just a dream."

"It wasn't a dream exactly."

"You're saying all that stuff really happened."

"Yes."

"But how?"

Frank thought for a minute. "It's hard to explain. Think of it like this: You've got two rooms, right? One room is the real world, the other one is your dream. There's a hall between the two rooms. That's the place where you're waking up or you're falling asleep. So, ordinarily, you're either in one room or the other. They're separate. You follow?"

"So far."

"Okay. But there's another room, a third room located between and above the other two. When you're asleep but not dreaming, your body and your brain slow way down and rest. But another part of you, the light, goes into the third room. The third room is a platform of power. The light can see everything from there and can act in ways that you have no knowledge of yet. When the light descends into the dream room, it's no ordinary dream you're having. Whatever happens there counts in both places. For example, if you die in that kind of dream, then some part of you really dies."

"Jesus."

"Yeah, it's pretty amazing, ain't it?"

"But I don't remember anything like a third room."

"Well, it's only *like* a room. There's no way to really describe it. For you, it was the web."

"And whose idea was that?"

"Yours."

"But Frank, it couldn't have been *my* idea. I mean, I would know wouldn't I?"

"Not necessarily. All I did was create the background, the possibilities. You picked out the specifics."

"But why a spider web?"

"I don't know. It's different with every person."

I looked at Frank. "Something's changed, hasn't it? You seem different. Everything looks different." I glanced around the room.

"Yeah," Frank said. "Something's changed. When you pass through the third room into the dream, you become one of us. You will always take that route into your dreams now. The old way is closed to you. Now, your life is your dreams, and your dreams are your life. To master either one, you have to master the other."

I felt drunk. I understood Frank's words, and yet they scattered like roaches when a light comes on. "There's something I've been wanting to ask you for a long time," I said.

"Go ahead."

"How come you never did anything with your life?"

The smile eased out of Frank's face. "What do you mean?"

"You've got abilities nobody else has. Why haven't you done anything with them?"

"You mean like my dad doing magic tricks on a stage?"

"You could be famous and rich."

"Did it make my dad rich or famous?"

"You could do something else, anything you wanted."

Frank stood up suddenly and inspected himself. He stood on one leg, pulled off his shoe and carefully studied his foot. Then he sucked in his stomach and looked down the front of his trousers. He undid the top button of his shirt and put his hand inside, feeling around.

I started laughing. "What are you doing?"

Frank stopped and looked at me. "Do you see anything wrong? I suddenly had the feeling something was wrong."

"No, you look okay to me."

"Good," Frank said with relief and sat back down.

"What's going on?"

"Are you really listening to me?"

"Yeah, I'm listening."

"You're something of a rare case. You've passed through the third room into the dream without being completely hollow."

I was trying to be patient. "I understand." I said. "I really do. I think I'm ready to get started." I stood up beside the bed, but Frank reached out, pulled me down and pinned me to the bed so easily and calmly that I stopped struggling immediately. In some sense, I still felt as small as an insect, vulnerable to attack, defenseless.

"What are you doing?" I said.

"I'm not getting through to you," Frank said.

"I heard every word you said."

"You're in a very dangerous phase, Chuck."

"Your mother told me you were like this." I could feel my mouth twisting into a sneer.

"Did she?" Frank removed his hand from my chest.

"She said you were a weak man just like your father. She said you were afraid to use your powers, a coward."

The smile came back to Frank's face. "Seems like you'd know by now that you can't hurt me." He pulled out another cigarette. "More to the point, it seems like you would stop wanting to hurt me." I wondered what had happened to the ashes and the butt from the first cigarette.

Frank exhaled a long, relaxed stream of smoke. "Do you want to know what my mother said about you?"

"Do I have a choice?"

"She said you weren't ready for any of this because all she could see when she looked inside you was your mother curled up like a moth in a cocoon. Not much room for any thing else in there."

I felt a familiar flash of pain inside. "What does my mother have to do with anything?"

"You tell me."

"My mother is dead, Frank. You're confusing me again. I thought I was beginning to figure it out."

"Let me make it clear for you. There are still obstacles, there's still a lack of vision on your part. When the power comes, confine your experimenting to this apartment. Understand?"

"Yeah, I understand." I didn't take my eyes off Frank now.

Frank looked at his watch. "It's time for you to pick up your papers. Get some clothes on."

I dressed while Frank watched silently with his arms folded. "What do you do with the ashes and the butts from your cigarettes? Do you stick them in your pocket, or just eat them?"

Frank made no response, kept watching.

I left the bedroom cautiously, scanning every corner of the living room. I still felt the presence of others in my apartment, but if they were there they were hiding under the paint. I went out the front door and Frank followed.

I turned around abruptly. "Listen. I don't want you coming back in my apartment unless you're invited. Understand?"

Frank nodded. I can't imagine what he must have thought of me then. He just looked at me, didn't say a word. I was stubborn, I admit it. Worse than stubborn. I was a fool.

Chapter Seven

As I DROVE away, I felt more confusion than ever. I was sure that my nervousness was brought on by exhaustion from the night before, and by hunger. There was an eeriness to every object I saw, as if each surface might suddenly be transformed.

Frank had sent me away early. I had an hour to kill before my papers would be ready, so I pulled into a Hardee's and bought a couple of burgers and some fries.

Part of my confusion obviously came from Frank himself. What did the man expect for Christ's sake? What was the power for if not to use and enjoy? I knew I wasn't going to be stupid about it. I knew that Frank had the knowledge and experience. I was going to try to live by Frank's rules, but I would only be bossed around up to a point. That was one of the main reasons I'd left home. I might be poor as an alley cat, but I was free as one too, and I wanted to keep it that way.

My strange mixture of feelings reminded me of something that had happened when I was a small boy, when my mother was still alive. My mother and father had not been getting along too well at that time. Nothing serious, but they didn't look happy when they were together. It was during the summer, and my mother had been out somewhere all morning, leaving me with Dave, the middle brother. I was sitting at the kitchen table eating a sandwich when I heard my mother drop her pocketbook and keys on the hall stand. She swept into the kitchen with a flourish and smiled at me expectantly. I laid my half-eaten sandwich on the plate and stared at her.

"Well?" she said, broadening her smile, holding her hands out at her sides palms up.

Like I said before, my mother was a beautiful woman. Even a seven-year-old boy could not fail to notice that. But she had done something to herself, and it took me a minute to see exactly what it was. I must've frowned because my mother's smile flattened and narrowed and her eyes dimmed and her hands came down to her sides.

"It can't be that bad." She drooped all of a sudden, leaning against the counter.

But it was pretty bad, I thought, still not sure enough of my feelings to respond to her. She was wearing an okay new dress, soft pink with white trim and it fit her neatly. But her hair had changed too, and it was a disaster. Instead of the long, shiny, slightly wavy hair that I loved, it was all bunched up on top of her head in tight little waves and curls. It looked solid, like artificial fruit. I could see her ears now with delicate pink earrings. But the worst thing was her smile. I'd never seen her smile that way. I watched it creeping back into her face. Sickening. It wasn't her real smile. For a few seconds I wondered if this was really my mother, the smile as artificial as her hair.

She walked over to me and put her hands on the sides of my face, cool as bed sheets on a winter night. She turned my face up to hers.

"You don't like it, huh? It's okay, you can tell the truth."

I swallowed hard. "No, I guess I don't like it."

"What don't you like?"

"I liked your hair better the other way. It was pretty."

She took her hands away and frowned. Then she walked back to the center of the room and when she turned around that smile was back on her face. She put her hands out beside her again like a model.

"Anything else?"

"Yeah. I don't like your smile."

The smile remained on her face, but a puzzled look came into her eyes and she cocked her head slightly. "Why not? What's wrong with my smile for God's sake?"

I should have taken that as a warning. She was not as religious as my father and brothers, but I'd never heard her say the word "God" irreverently. She was less herself that day than I'd realized.

"It makes me feel weird," I said. "It doesn't look like it fits right on your face." I watched the smile disappear from her face and it made me feel better. I added, "Who are you trying to fool anyway?"

It was something I'd heard people say on TV, and it just jumped out of my mouth before I could gauge its worth. But when I saw her stiffen and saw the change in her eyes, I knew that what I'd said meant more than I realized.

She came across the room in two steps, grabbed me by the back of my shirt, yanked me out of the booth and marched me to my room.

"Two hours." Her hand clenched the doorknob. "And I don't want to hear a sound."

"But you said I could go over to Bill's house when you got back!"

"Not today you aren't."

"But what did I do wrong?"

"I won't have you treating me with disrespect. There are some things I will put up with, but that's not one of them."

"You told me to tell the truth."

"There's a right way and a wrong way to tell the truth. Especially when you're talking to your mother. Not another sound." She pulled the door shut.

I stomped around the room. I was being punished for nothing. I crumpled up pieces of paper and threw them at the windows as hard as I could, careful not to make any noise. I kicked the side of my bed and jammed my big toe, using the pain to fuel my anger. I flopped down on the bed, tensing every muscle in my body, a perverse isometric grimace on my face. Fiercely twisting the corners of my pillow, I bit down as hard as I could on the foam, salty tears making spots on the pillowcase. Suddenly a cold chill went through me as I saw someone in the corner of my eye. I turned my head, and it was my mother not five feet away with her arms folded over her chest. She was absolutely still, and I felt frozen too in her stare, though I could feel the heat of guilt and shame flooding my neck and cheeks. A glint of fire was still in her eyes, but at least that strange smile was gone.

"I'm glad you told me the truth," she said. She headed for the door, but turned back around. "No need to bust a gut over this." She closed the door behind her.

I lay on the bed mired in my misery for the rest of the afternoon. She never came back to tell me when my two hours were up.

Later that evening, my mother's new dress and new hair were a big success, my two brothers dutifully telling her how beautiful she was, my father, still in his coat and tie, giving her an especially long kiss. But I noticed that she didn't display her new smile that night.

After everyone had gone to bed, I could hear my mother and father laughing. Then the sounds they made were harder to hear.

I PICKED UP my burger, but put it back down on the paper wrapper without taking a bite. I was having to work very hard not to cry. Why was I being so emotional all of a sudden? In the eight remaining years of her life, I never once saw my mother smile in that strange way again.

But now I had the same odd feeling in the pit of my stomach that her smile had given me, and I didn't know why. There was a sheen on the surface of things that sickened me. The whole world looked artificial. It had started when I awakened from my strange dreams and Frank had come into my room with that big grin. Now I was supposed to have the powers, but I couldn't make them work. I tried to make the plastic salt shaker slide across the table, but nothing happened. The idea that I'd had about myself for a long time was even stronger now, that I was a child in a world where I was forced to pretend I was a man.

I drove slower than usual as I headed toward *The Sun*, feeling that the road might be pulled out from under me any minute. When I turned into the loading area of *The Sun*, my sense that everything had changed was magnified tenfold. Even *The Sun* itself, a great block of a building, had a subtle glimmer today in the dimness of an overcast sky. I pulled into my usual slot at the dock and was immediately put on guard by something I could only define as silence, though there was plenty of noise around. There was the rumble of the conveyors upstairs that brought bundles of papers to the chutes. Coming from deep inside the building was the broader pounding and rumbling of the presses and the folders and the machines that wrapped the bundles tightly in wire, and the sound of those bundles being dropped into truck beds or thrown onto stacks at the edge of the dock, the sound of vehicle doors opening and shutting, engines turning over, firing up.

But beneath all of this there was a suffocating silence, and I soon figured out what it was. Thirty or forty people were working in a small area, and not a word was passing between them.

The Wallaces were in the slot next to me, and old man Wallace leaned against his truck door. His two sons were in the bed, Jeff taking the toss from the chute man and passing the bundle back to John who stacked it carefully. When they finished, the load would be higher than the cab and it had to be tight to avoid any losses overboard. They carried several thousand papers, had at least a dozen paper boys running neighborhood routes for them, delivered the rest themselves, and made enough money to support themselves comfortably.

I liked the Wallaces. Old man Wallace had named his sons Jeff and John because of the J's. He liked the idea that all the men in his family had names that began with "J". He was James, his brother was Joshua, and his own father had been Jake. I had been over to the Wallaces for dinner several times. I liked the boys, who were a few years older than me, still unmarried, and wild in an old fashioned, good ol' boy sort of way. They spent a lot of time hiking and rock climbing in the nearby mountains. And all three of them liked to talk. It was always hard for me to get a word in edgewise. Old man Wallace told some great war stories and other tales from his youth. He'd been career military, retired with the rank of Colonel but never used it as a title like most men would.

Being with the Wallaces reminded me of my own motherless home with two brothers, only without the religious pressure, and without the tension of those memories of my mother and her death. Mrs. Wallace had also died when she was young, from injuries she'd received in a plane crash. It had been hard on them at first, but time had passed and they were doing fine now.

But today the Wallaces were silent. And Phieffer on the other side of them, loading his Toyota pickup, and Mrs. Posselt next to him with her station wagon, and everyone else up and down the dock was silent. I stood there for a while and watched them from my own place of silence. At first I figured they were all just wrapped up in their private thoughts, but then I changed my mind. I noticed that every time Jeff turned to John to hand him a bundle, their eyes met and something passed between them. What made this strange to me was that it happened with every single exchange, exactly the same way every time. And the others were doing it too. Wallace, Phieffer, Mrs. Posselt, the other carriers and the men working on the dock, were all having these little moments of silent communication with each other. Their eyes would meet, and then they would get this subtle, knowing look on their faces, the possibility of a smile flickering there, and then they would move on. Then suddenly I heard a loud whistle. It was Williams on the dock holding one of my bundles. As Williams passed it down to me, I avoided his eyes. I felt a little embarrassed by all of this, maybe even intimidated, and each time Williams returned with one of my bundles I would just keep my eyes on that bundle and dodge the whole problem.

When I opened my car door, I felt a friendly slap on my shoulder. I turned and looked into the kindly stare of Richard Phieffer.

"Whoa boy," Phieffer said as if he were calming a skittish colt. He'd been at *The Sun* longer than me and had developed an excellent thousand paper route in one of the suburban areas of town. He took on two or three boys to cover part of it and he did the rest himself. About thirty, he had the steady calmness of a man who had seen and done a lot of things. He'd been a great football player, but he broke his leg badly in a car accident during his sophomore year. He dropped out of school and disappeared for a while. Old man Wallace always liked to say that was when he'd "got his head screwed on straight." But I, even though I liked Phieffer, had always been a little suspicious. Why would a man who could use his reputation as an athlete to go into business or politics sell newspapers seven days a week? Why hadn't Phieffer finished his education which was paid for with a scholarship? These questions pulsed in me as I met the curious gaze of Phieffer's pale green eyes, his hand still firmly gripping my shoulder.

"Are you okay?" Phieffer asked.

"Yeah, sure, I'm fine. Why shouldn't I be?"

"Frank said you were out cold for twelve hours."

"Frank told you that?"

He nodded.

"What else did he tell you?" I wanted to move out from under that big hand. It reminded me of the patronizing shoulder squeeze of the preacher back home at my father's church. But I forced myself to be still.

"Listen now. It's only natural to be a little nervous for a while." His eyes never moved from mine, reaching inside me, probing, asking a question, not getting the answer.

"Why should I be nervous?"

Phieffer stroked his chin with two fingers and blinked his eyes. "No reason I don't guess."

But he kept probing with those eyes. I had been an athlete too. I'd been small, wiry, quick, clever, stronger than I looked. But in Phieffer's presence I had an almost stifling sense of the other man's awesome physical power. Phieffer was not overwhelmingly tall at 6'2", but he was broad and flawlessly muscled from his neck to his feet. I knew that he worked out a lot and ran five or six miles a day and was probably the best handball player in the city if not in the state. I felt imprisoned as I stood there under Phieffer's hand, time dripping by like the run-off of a slow-burning candle.

"I'd better get going on my route."

"Yeah, right," Phieffer said, removing his hand from my shoulder.

"See you later." I climbed into my car and shut the door.

"Listen," Phieffer said through the open window. "Why don't we hit one of the bars tonight?"

I looked up at him. I'd gone out with Phieffer three or four times before, and it had been okay. Phieffer had a way of attracting people, especially good-looking women. I had met some I liked this way, but I hadn't followed through on it. I just kept thinking about Sandy. Besides, why would an attractive woman be interested in a paper boy?

"Okay. Why not?"

THIS WAS ANOTHER one of those days when the route seemed to take forever. Sometimes I regretted the additional streets that Frank had connected to the route. I wasn't sure the extra time and hassle were worth the money. And collecting had become a nightmare. I was beginning to think I didn't want to do this much longer. Almost anything would be better, even if it was harder work. Besides, if I was really going to have the powers that Frank said I would, there would be a lot of ways to make money. As I was rolling and throwing, I tried to activate the light, to feel it sliding out of me like an extra invisible hand in the space before me, but it wasn't there. I would have to wait.

It was five o'clock by the time I got home. When I opened the door I was struck by the same silent atmosphere in my rooms that had been at *The Sun*, as if the surfaces of this, my most private place, had somehow changed. Standing in my doorway, listening intently, I remembered that Frank had been here earlier, had probably spent the night here. I didn't like the idea of someone digging around in my things. I closed the door and took another step, then stopped again listening for the slightest sound, the motion of breath, but all I heard was the tiny motor of my electric clock, almost like the purring of a cat. When I'd finally convinced myself that no one else was here, I went back to my room and pulled on a sweater. It had started to get cold.

I came back into the living room, raked the pile of clothes and paperbacks from my chair and sat before my desk. It suddenly occurred to me that this was the moment I'd been waiting for, that the power would come to me in this room, now. That's the way Frank would have set it up. The power would emerge in this room where I felt safe and nothing could go wrong.

I stretched the adjustable arm of my lamp and turned it on, the small stone with a tiny piece of paper on top in the center of the circle of light. I had not attempted to move the piece of paper in a week, and now I felt that the groove of concentration was gone. But it didn't matter. I could call it back up. I knew that this moment was the culmination of a long process, that I had earned the fulfillment of that promise of power that had been in the air ever since the day that Frank had first walked into this very room, causing the door to close without touching it. I remembered that first day on the route, the way Frank had thrown the papers with a touch and accuracy that couldn't be believed or explained. I smiled. That had been the first real bait Frank had dangled before me, and I'd swallowed it whole. Following Frank's directions as best I could, I'd sacrificed my life with Sandy, at least temporarily, and my peace of mind, to reach this particular moment.

And now that I was here, I was surprised at myself. I felt none of the excitement or nervousness that I'd expected. Instead there was only the comfortable desire to savor the moment. I would receive my power with a calmness and control that would make Frank proud.

Still, some effort was necessary, some degree of concentration. I closed my eyes and began to empty my mind, disintegrating each thought and image until a quality of silence swept through me, my mind becoming a vacuum drawing to a focal point all the forces of my will. I opened my eyes, staring at that small piece of paper on the stone. It lifted, dangling above the stone like a dead leaf hanging from a web. I noticed no unusual sensations beyond the slight tugging in the pit of my stomach that had always accompanied my witnessing one of these events. I flew the piece of paper all around the room, the fluttering of a moth. I seemed to have complete control. I withdrew my effort and it dropped to the floor in a flickering swirl.

I returned to the stone. It lifted immediately, with no more effort than the piece of paper. I began to laugh out loud as I propelled it around the room like a small, remote-controlled rocket. A wave of sheer joy coursed through my body. Tears trickled down my face. Finally, I reeled the stone in, cupped it in my hand for a moment, then put it in my pocket. It would be a talisman to remind me of my special place in the world. Then I sat back in my chair, locked my hands behind my head, and began to experiment. I lifted a big pile of clothes and paperbacks and assorted trash up into a whirlwind. Nothing I attempted required a greater effort than the stone until I started moving the furniture, and then there was a sharper ridge of tension stretching from my eyes down to that same place in my stomach. Without moving from my chair, I rearranged everything in my living room. I played like this for over an hour.

THE PHOENIX WAS not the kind of place Phieffer had taken me before. This was more of a restaurant than a bar, with heavy wooden tables and chairs and tropical plants hanging from the ceiling. Old standards played in the background, Sinatra and Ella Fitzgerald, the kind of place you might take a date if you could afford it.

"What are we doing here?"

"You don't like it?" Phieffer worked his shoulders and neck, loosening up like a boxer in his corner before the first bell.

We slid into a booth. Phieffer had already retrieved a couple of the local draft beers. "I like it okay, but I sure as hell can't afford it. One or two of these drafts and I'm done for the night."

"Don't worry about it. I'm buying. So enjoy."

"I would, except where's the rock-and-roll and sexy girls and all that? I mean, this is the kind of place that rich guys who go to church come to drink."

Phieffer laughed. "You've got some funny ideas Chuck."

"I was kind of hoping for more of a celebration tonight."

Phieffer ran his hand over his face, and the laugh disappeared. "I had some things to talk over with you." He tried to muffle the serious tone, but failed. "But we can do that later," he said more cheerfully. "What've you got to celebrate?"

I lifted my beer and took a slow sip. Just how much did Phieffer know? I didn't want to give away information that would cause trouble for Frank, or myself. I set my beer down, stared at it like it was a crystal ball.

"It's alright," Phieffer said finally. "I know all about Frank. You can talk to me. I can tell something's wrong."

"Nothing's wrong. In fact, everything's right. You want me to demonstrate?"

Like the rest of Phieffer's body, his face was all bone and muscle, as if he could ram a hole right through you with his head. The muscles in his jaw and temples flexed. "If you mean what I think you mean..."

"You and Frank are two of a kind, you know that? Always looking for something to worry about, always afraid to enjoy what you have." Phieffer's ninja-fierce face made me laugh out loud. It was interesting to note that he let me have my laugh. He settled back and simply observed me, as if he'd thrown cool water on whatever reaction he might have had inside. "I've got a question for you," I said, recovering. "Just how much money *do* you have?"

"My dad's a wealthy man, most of it from oil and steel. I'm talking fifty million more or less."

"Jesus."

"That's my dad. When I graduated from high school he gave me a million bucks. I could live pretty good off the interest and dividends, but I don't use much of it. I give my checking account a little boost every now and then."

"I don't get it. Why does a guy in your situation peddle papers?"

"Well, that's a tough question."

"You can handle it."

"By now I was supposed to be in the last years of a great pro football career. I was going to retire before thirty-five and go into TV commentary. It could've happened that way, I was the type. I mean, I was high school all American two years in a row. In college, I was the top Freshman tailback in the country. I thought I could see my future stretching out like a red carpet in front of me as far as I could think about it. I knew I'd be considered for the Heisman in my junior year. Then my real future started happening. Do you really want to hear about this?"

"Yeah, I do."

"It was my sophomore year, the Sunday evening after the second game. The papers were full of pictures of me running downfield breaking tackles. I'd done an interview on national TV for CBS that afternoon. People were already noticing how good I was in front of the camera. Anyway, four of us on the team went out just cruising around, and we were broadsided by some psycho on drugs. Must've been going 60 or 70 when he hit us. Bull Braddock was driving, all American center. Took the impact right on his door. Big as he was he was practically broke in half. Sammy Walsh, back-up quarterback, was dead with a broken neck, never mind his other injuries. Rick Plumly, cornerback, who'd been in the back seat with me, miraculously survived. He lost his left eye and had about a hundred broken bones. It took him a year to get to where he could walk with a cane. I still have a drink with him every once in a while.

"I guess I was the only one who came out of that mess relatively unhurt. I had a broken leg and a concussion, but I was going to be normal again, in time. Thought I might even get back to football."

"Did the leg just not heal right or something?"

"No, the leg healed great, considering how bad it was broken. And I had the best doctors and trainers a rich father could buy. I was out of my cast and working out by the first of the year. Worked my ass off all winter, spring and summer. A lot of people don't remember this, but I was back with the team at the start of my junior year. I'd lost about half a second in the hundred and I just couldn't seem to make it up. That may not sound like much, but in that league that's the half second that makes the difference. And just as bad, I'd lost mobility. That leg would always be a little stiffer, a little slower to react. I'd been reduced to a mediocre power back, three yards and a cloud of dust. The coaches were talking about putting me on defense as a linebacker, but the idea didn't sit right with me. My dream of being an NFL superstar fizzled into nothing. I got to feeling real sorry for myself."

"So what did you do?"

"I just quit like the spoiled brat I was. Spent about three years doing whatever drugs I could find and getting laid. I was miserable and fat and stoned. That was my life. My father tried to bring me into his business, but it didn't feel right. When I told him I couldn't do it, he got so mad he disowned me. He couldn't take away what he'd already given me, but he could keep me from ever getting any more. I tried to explain it to him. I wanted to do something on my own, but I didn't know what and I didn't seem to be getting any closer to it." Phieffer smiled, took a sip of his beer. "That's when I met Frank."

"Oh shit ..."

"What?"

"Every time you talk about Frank your voice changes, did you know that? You start sounding real reverent, like you were talking about Jesus or something. Yeah, like you were witnessing for Jesus. I've been around that kind of thing enough to know what it sounds like."

Phieffer sat back in his seat for a second as if he were giving the idea its due. "I think you're imagining things. Besides, nobody is more a follower of Frank than you are."

"I'm not following Frank."

"There's no point in arguing about it ..."

"I don't think I can handle any more of this without another beer." I pushed my empty glass to the middle of the table. Phieffer bought another round. "Anyway," I said, "I know what you're going to say: Frank changed your whole life. Right?"

Phieffer nodded slowly. "Yeah, that's right. He's changed your life too."

"Listen, I learn what I can, and I use it. But I'm always my own man."

"All I know is Frank helped me turn my life around, and he's doing the same for you. You might try showing a little gratitude."

"If you call throwing papers turning your life around, that's pretty pitiful. Some big favor he did you."

"It's the first time in my life I've done something for other people and earned an honest wage for it. It gives me a basic connection with things."

"Yeah, it's basic all right. The thing is, you don't have to live on that small income. You've got all the money you want. You come to places like this."

"The job is just a small part of it Chuck. But you don't know what I'm talking about, do you?"

I smiled knowingly as I'd seen the others do at *The Sun*. "The powers."

Phieffer shook his head but said nothing, just kept staring at me.

I drank some of my beer, trying to outwait him, but the silence stretched on.

"How many like us are there?" I said.

Phieffer had become so still I wasn't sure he was breathing, and his eyes studied me the way Frank's mother's had. Like a bird looking at a bug in the grass. "I'm not sure, but the number would start with everybody in the circulation department at *The Sun*."

"What do you mean by everybody?"

"Just what I said. You should be seeing that for yourself by now."

"Yeah, I did notice something strange there today. But, I mean, *all* of them?"

Phieffer nodded. "They're all at one stage or another."

"What about upstairs, the reporters, the secretaries, the guys running the press?"

"No, just circulation."

"Jesus. Still, that's a lot."

"It's the largest concentration of our kind in a thousand years."

"Are there others, away from *The Sun*?"

"Some, scattered around the world. And some children with them, growing up . . . you know . . . in the knowledge."

"Frank's mother?"

"A very powerful lady."

"Yeah, she scared the shit out of me. But I still don't understand this stuff about *The Sun*. What about the owners?"

"Frank owns *The Sun*. It's been in his family for fifty years. Frank's father was never involved with it of course, but his Uncle

Marcus took it over from old man Posner when it was still a very small operation. Marcus had no children, and he was always taking Frank under his wing because he didn't approve of that nomadic circus life that Frank's father was leading. Frank inherited controlling stock in the business, but his own involvement in the paper has always been with circulation. Just wasn't interested in managing the paper from the top, not the executive type I guess. He's been running the paper in his own way for fifteen years, always throwing up a pretty thick legal smoke screen to keep his name clear of it on the surface. Sharpe takes care of the business end of things for the most part, and Frank likes being in control of circulation, where he can bring each new carrier, one by one, into the tribe. It's a pretty amazing set-up I think. *The Sun* is the center we all come back to. It's our home."

"Well, you can cut me out of this 'we' you keep throwing around."

"You're part of us whether you like it or not. There's no point in being stupid, Chuck. Whatever you do will affect us all and vice versa. We just want to make sure you understand. Quite frankly, you make us a little nervous."

"You're trying to tell me I went through all that shit for nothing. What good are the powers if I can't use them?"

"The fact that you have to ask worries me."

I slid out of the booth, took a five out of my wallet and tossed it on the table. "This is for the beers and the advice, which is about what it's worth."

I walked out of the bar. I had considered a showdown of powers, like two super heroes in a DC comic, but thought better of it. All I'd done so far was move a few things around in my apartment. Phieffer had had more time with the powers and might be stronger. I wandered into a couple more bars, but ended up drinking alone, my good mood in ruins. I hated to admit it, but I'd let Phieffer get to me. I knew I'd been a jerk with him, but I was feeling so good after moving that rock around. Phieffer was such a muscle-bound square. I had earned my powers, and I was determined not to let Phieffer and Frank make me feel guilty or obligated to them in any way. I sensed that I'd barely scratched the surface of these new abilities. If I could make objects move by an act of will, what else could I do? One thing was for sure. My powers would enable me to overcome my lack of education and connections. I didn't see anything wrong with that.

I try not to think too poorly of the person I was in those days. It's not that I was stupid or vicious, though the acts I found myself compelled to commit might lead one to that conclusion. It's just that when we're young, it's pretty hard sometimes to see past our own private game of pick-up sticks.

Chapter Eight

I STRETCHED OUT on my bed, the excitement of those past two days throbbing in my body like a fever. Everything was different now. Even the darkness of my room glistened as I moved my eyes over the familiar walls and furniture. I knew that my sleep of the night before was not real sleep, that my dream had been more than dream, that I had traveled through the third room into Frank's mysterious world leaving my old life behind like a shed skin.

But all was not as it should be. If both Frank and Phieffer had noticed, there must be something to it. Still, I had to act on what I felt. And what I felt most strongly about was Sandy. Now that I really had something going for a change, I wanted her back in my life. That would be the main order of business, finding Sandy, explaining everything to her—no, proving it to her, because that's what her scientist's mind would require—then starting over. But first I had to get some rest.

I craved a deep and dreamless sleep, though I didn't expect it. For the past year my sleep had been haunted by the recurring dream of the spider and for years before that the dream about my mother in the hospital. I would try an old trick of mine. Sometimes if I could make myself think of only one thing as I was falling asleep, that's what I would dream of. I thought of Sandy. I saw her clearly, sitting on a couch beside me. We were talking.

"Whaddya say, kiddo?"

But this wasn't Sandy's voice. And then it wasn't Sandy's face I was seeing.

"Whaddya say, kiddo? Let's go out to Edgerton Lake." She flashed that playful smile of hers. I didn't know how I'd managed it, but I was stuck at home alone with her again on a hot Sunday afternoon in June. Where was everybody else?

"But it's not even finished yet. It's closed to the public," I said.

"I know, but Sam won't care if we test the water. We'll have the whole place to ourselves."

I shrugged my shoulders. I had nothing better to do. If my mother wanted to go off and get herself arrested for trespassing or shot at by half-blind, half-crazy Sam Edgerton, it was no skin off my nose. I was just a kid. People don't arrest or shoot kids. I could sit on the beach and enjoy the spectacle and shake my head and wonder why she had to be so different. Why not more like Mrs. Walker across the street? A chubby, amiable woman who liked to drive the neighborhood kids around to movies and museums. Why did my mother have to be the slender politician that everybody either loved or hated? She was always trying to change everything, at school, at city hall, even at home.

So we took the long drive into the country. Mostly she talked and I listened. I tried to turn the radio on, but she wouldn't let me. Instead I had to listen to an impassioned and no doubt inaccurate lecture on physics.

"Do you know what an atom is?"

"I'm not in the first grade you know."

"Okay smart guy, what's an atom?"

"Do I have to do this? It's summer and I'm supposed to be resting my brain."

"Yes, you have to answer. I want to see if they're teaching you anything down at that school."

I shook my head in disgust, but decided it wasn't worth an argument. "Okay. An atom is the smallest building block that everything is made of."

"Yeah, and what is an atom made of?"

"Nothing. If it's the smallest building block, then it can only be made of itself."

"Smart guy. Come on. Let's not make this a game of semantics."

"Well, it has a nucleus . . ."

"Ummm hmmm . . ."

" . . . and a bunch of little specks of energy called electrons flying around it in orbits."

"And what else?"

"Uh, the nucleus contains little particles called protons and neutrons."

"Keep going."

"That's all I really know. I mean, they've discovered some other sub-atomic particles, but we haven't studied them. Oh, I remember. The protons and neutrons are made of quarks, I think."

"Okay, so not counting the particles you've named and the ones you don't know the names of, what's left? What else is an atom made of?"

"I don't follow you. That's all there is."

"No, think about it. What else?"

I stared at my hands and thought about it. Just like in school. "Nothing."

"Right!" She slapped my knee. "Nothing. Just empty space. Ninety-nine percent of an atom, at least, is just empty space."

"I'm not sure about this. It's an energy field or something. They've decided it's particles or waves, I can't remember."

"No, what I'm saying is true. All those little electrons are flying around in a space as black and empty as outer space."

"But outer space isn't really empty either, not exactly empty . . ." I started, but she gave me her impatient frown, and I gave in, as always. "Okay, if you say so."

"I do. And you know what that means?"

"No, what?"

"That everything is made of ninety-nine percent nothing."

"Huh?"

"That's right. If atoms are ninety-nine percent empty space, and everything is made of atoms, then everything is mostly space. For example, this steering wheel," she thumped it, "is made of mostly empty space."

"Then how come you can't put your hand through it?"

"I can." She put her hand through the center opening of the wheel with a silly grin.

"Not *that* part."

Laughing, she pulled her hand out of the wheel. "Well, there's a reason. It has to do with how fast all those little particles are moving, filling in the space. Or maybe it's the interaction of all those electrical forces. I'm not sure I can explain it. Why don't you look it up? Anyway, there's a more important part. You want to hear it?"

"Do I have a choice?"

"Not really."

"In that case I'd love to hear it."

"It's like this. Our solar system is like an atom, with the sun as nucleus and the planets as revolving electrons. Right?"

"Yeah, I've heard this before. The binding forces are different, but they're similar."

"Of course. It's obvious. Now just like an atom, the solar system is made mostly of empty space. And what's in that empty space?"

"Nothing."

"Wrong."

"If it's empty space, how can something be in it?"

"Think about it. If you're out there floating around among the planets and such, what's there?"

"Well, you'd see the stars."

"Is it the actual stars you'd see?"

"No, you'd see their light."

"Right. No matter where you'd drift to in this giant atom we live in, or in any of the adjoining atoms of our galaxy, you'd always be able to see the light of the sun or the other stars and objects reflecting that light. So the solar system and the galaxy and everywhere else in the universe is filled with this fine dust of light. And the space in atoms, which are tiny models of these bigger forms, is filled with light too. Which means that everything is made mostly of light."

"Wait a minute. It's a pretty big jump from galaxies to atoms."

"Not really. The same laws apply everywhere."

"Mom?" She glanced from the road to look at me and smiled. She loved it when I allowed myself to call her "Mom."

"Yes?" she said, stretching it out.

"I think this is all old news. They've discovered all sorts of other stuff now."

"Like what?"

"I can't remember all of it. The laws for big things like galaxies aren't the same as they are for little things, like quarks. That's what got Einstein so mad. His theory of relativity didn't work too well for the little things. They didn't teach this in school. I read about it in some magazine."

"I should've known. I think we have the same sources." She nodded toward something out her window. "Open the gate?"

We pulled off the blacktop into a narrow dirt road. I jumped out of the car, lifted the loop of bailing twine, and swung the gate open. The lake itself was at the end of this mile-long road penetrating the oldest forest in the state. At least that's what the naturalist at the museum said. We drove slowly, avoiding the large holes in the road and the rabbits and squirrels that seemed to delight in darting across in front of us, sometimes stopping abruptly in the middle to dance in a panic of indecision before disappearing again in the underbrush. Hardwoods dominated here and teemed with the short flights and warning chirps of birds.

"Just think, all of this is made out of light," she said.

There was no point in arguing with her. She liked the idea too much to let logic or facts get in the way. It was all nonsense, of course, but an attractive nonsense, especially on such a warm summer day with so much brightness showing itself as if in proof. All she would have to do is point and say, "See?!" And on this day I did see, the tops of trees moving in a slight breeze, playing with the slanted rays of the sun like the games that children play on their hands with bright colored string.

The lake and the area surrounding it were deserted, just as she'd predicted. Sam Edgerton planned to open the lake to the public sometime that summer and had already started building a small pavilion with a rec room, showers and a concession. He'd brought in truck loads of white sand for a beach and had put up swings and picnic tables in a grove of oaks overlooking the lake.

In a small clearing at the end of the road, we stripped down to bathing suits and tossed our clothes into the back seat. I couldn't help but marvel at her secretly, better looking at thirty-five than the high school girls I stared at in the drug-store soda shop or at football games, so slender for the mother of three. We tiptoed down the grassy slope, wary of the big pieces of green glass from a broken bottle of whiskey. We walked over the bare ground that would be beach, between two mountains of white sand to the water's edge. It was a pretty lake surrounded by those woods that had been left to themselves so long. Even the hunters had been kept away. And to old Sam's credit, as few trees as possible had been taken to make the lake accessible.

I thought this had to be the quietest place I'd ever been, so far from the sound of cars and human voices. The low sun made a bright spot on the water that drew a flame-like arrow to our feet. Out on the lake all but one of the twenty canoes Sam had brought in were drifting freely in the soft breeze.

"Kids," she said.

"If anybody comes, they'll think we did it."

She turned to me for a second, eyes serene with the beauty and quiet of this place. "It's okay. We'll tell them we didn't."

Then she made a shallow dive, the water pulling her hair back like a strong wind. She surfaced and stood facing me in water that came to her chest. "Come on, it'll be dark soon." She swam gracefully out toward a platform that supported a low dive and a high dive, thirty yards or so from the shore.

I waded out to mid-calf, sucking air back through my teeth. I watched her pull herself up on the platform and turn to look for me, shading her eyes with both hands, her form at that distance and in that unusual light a dark leaf standing upright and unmoving in the breeze as if by some miracle.

"What are you waiting for?" she called.

"It's too cold," I called back.

"Spring fed," her voice rang out over the water, "you'll get used to it. What would your girlfriend think?" She started up the metal steps to the high dive.

"I don't have one," I called. Then I dove impulsively into the water, shaking off the chill, letting out with a big yell as I surfaced. I swam hard, knowing it would help me adjust to the cold, help me move faster through the pockets of colder water. I saw her high above me on the board, going through that slow, graceful ritual from her diving days. Then she lifted from the board and seemed to float through the long arc of a swan dive, barely moving the water as she entered.

I climbed onto the platform and sat down on the edge dangling my feet in the water, my body already warmed up from the exertion of swimming, the fat red sun sitting on the tops of trees, pressing its warmth like a soft towel against my face and chest. I had to admit that it was a perfect afternoon to be at Edgerton Lake. I heard her climbing from the water behind me, heard her wet feet patting the boards. Then she was standing over me, dripping on my neck and back.

"You're not just going to sit there are you?"

"Why not?"

"You're going to waste the light. We don't have that much time."

"But I'm enjoying it like this."

"Have you been practicing your dive over at Billy's?"

"Some."

"Let me see."

"Now?"

"Ummm hmmm."

"Do I have to?"

"Yes. Now come on. I'll be your coach."

She coaxed me onto the low board, had me bounce around to get the feel of it. Then, standing below and beside me, she instructed me on posture, lifting and opening my chest, holding my shoulders square, eyes straight ahead, hands just so at my side. She put her hands on my feet, her left hand up the inside of my leg to the calf and squeezed.

"You've got to use your toes and this muscle right here." She squeezed again. "Make the board give you all the thrust it has. This is no time for being shy. You've got to be aggressive and really go for it. Okay?"

"Okay."

She stepped away from me. So many times since I'd first learned to swim as an infant, I'd stood like this in the spotlight of her eyes. I watched my breath, wanting to time it right with that first forward lean of my upper body, believing that my carefully measured strides would take me to just the right spot at the end of the board. They did, and the board gave me a powerful lift up and out to that instant of grace in the air over water when my mind and body seemed left behind forever, a niche that stretched into an ocean of bright silence and space. I slipped in so smoothly the water seemed to unfold for me, the deep plunge of an arrow straight in. I allowed myself to cruise into the cold depths until the pressure in my head became uncomfortable, then I turned and kicked, bringing myself back to the surface of time and place.

"Bravo!" She whistled and applauded. "Tens straight across, except for the Russian judge who gave you a 9.9."

"It did feel good," I said, climbing out of the water.

"It was perfect."

Then she led me through a series of the more difficult dives which I rarely attempted without her help.

"You're really good, you know that? With a little time and effort you could be competitive, maybe even a champion."

"Naaahhh." I shook my head. "It would be too much trouble. Besides, you're the diving champ of the family. I'm gonna do something else."

"Yeah? Like what?"

"I don't know yet."

"You want to try some of those on the high board?"

"Not today. You go ahead."

I almost never dove from the high board when I was with her. If I did, I knew that she would coach me, that she would push me toward a more serious commitment to diving. I liked diving a lot, but it didn't feel right to follow in her footsteps like that. Besides, diving was not really a big sport with my friends or with anyone I knew. There wasn't much point in it.

So I sat on the edge of the platform and she went through her repertoire of dives. It seemed to me, watching her that day, that she must've been as good as she'd been when she was a teenager trying out for the Olympic team. She would've made it, too, except that she broke her left ankle. Four years after that she was already married with a kid and one in the works. So much for big-time dreams.

Who needed dreams anyway on a day like this? The sun was mostly behind the trees, but the sky and its few white puffs of cloud were filled with light. The air was warm and the lake was a dark, peaceful green stolen from the trees that stood at its rim forever contemplating that final, uprooting plunge. And everywhere, moving as slowly as freighters at a great distance on the ocean's horizon, empty canoes drifted from bank to bank. For some reason, as I sat there, I felt especially good, the water barely cool on my dangling feet, my mind as quiet and aimless as one of those canoes, the only sound was her climbing up from the water, wet feet patting the planks, slight creaking of the ladder, the muted twang of the board, her entry into water as quiet as a pillow landing on a bed.

Then I saw something long and tinged with yellow light in the water deep beneath my feet. It was rising fast and before I could move, erupted from the surface, threw water on me, pulled itself onto the platform beside me, laughing, long brown hair slick as an otter's.

"You should see the look on your face," she said, still laughing. "You must've been in dreamland."

"Yeah, I must've been." I stared at her for a minute, wide-eyed, the water pouring off her body onto mine.

The playful look on her face changed and she put her arms around me. "Is everything okay? What are you thinking about so hard?"

"Nothing much." I looked away.

"No trouble with your friends?"

"No."

"Problems with your girlfriend?"

"Definitely not. I don't have a girlfriend."

"That could be a problem too."

"No. It's not a problem. I don't really *want* a girlfriend yet."

"What about Alicia?"

I looked at her in disbelief. "Alicia is *not* my girlfriend."

"That's not what *I* heard."

"You heard wrong."

"Okay, okay. I didn't mean to butt in. You just looked like you were down, that's all."

I hated it when she got concerned, which was almost always, because she thought she had to hug me. This was especially bad, with her arms and legs against me, that wet, yellow suit stuck to her as tight as her own skin, her nipples showing through as clean as if she were naked. Why would she wear something like that where people could see her? She pressed against my shoulder, tightened her arms around me, and, missing her intended target, kissed me on the eye.

"Yuck! You're wet!"

"Yes. Water does that to you."

She held me for a long moment, looking at me with eyes containing something that I couldn't see because my neck was frozen solid and wouldn't turn my head. My whole body stiffened in her embrace.

"Do you know how much I love you?" Her breath was hot against my ear.

The peaceful silence from a moment before swelled in my throat now like a giant pill that wouldn't go down, or come back up either. Finally, I managed to turn to her in a sudden jerk. Her eyes were full of emotion, on the verge of tears.

"It's not always easy for mothers and sons, is it?" she said.

I shook my head. My breath came in heavy, irregular bursts. Why was I so angry? Or afraid? Or whatever it was, this feeling that was trying to gnaw its way out from the inside.

She stood up and walked to the other side of the platform, staring out across the lake. It seemed like every minute I spent with her was complicated and hard. So why did I let myself get caught with her alone like this? I had to admit to myself that I hated her. I hated the way my father was always working out with weights, always strutting around to keep the other men away, even at church. She had turned him into a fool.

Everything slowed down. I was trapped with her on this island in the middle of a lake at the edge of darkness, this amazing woman whose eyes were level with mine when we stood face-to-face, but who was stronger than I was, who had given birth to me and yet seemed more foreign than any other human being I could imagine. Couldn't she see the way I looked at her, the way I hated her?

Finally she breathed out heavily and shook her head. It was really getting dark now and she looked for another minute at the wall of trees across the lake.

"It's getting late. We'd better go," she said.

She dove into the lake and swam.

That was where it ended, with me standing on that platform in first darkness and her moving through the water toward that half-made beach, only the back of her head and upper shoulders and the slow, rhythmic motion of her arms visible on the surface.

Out of all those years, out of all the times with her I could have chosen, this was the one that I wanted to keep. The one that was the truest vision of her. It brought back her beauty, my confusion when I was with her, the fact that I had hated her even before she got so sick and withered away. I lay in my bed with my hands behind my head, eyes wide open. I wasn't sure I'd slept at all, wasn't sure that what I'd often called a dream wasn't anything more or less than a memory, the truth as far as I could recall it through ten years time. Or maybe it was more dream than I wanted to think, colored by some part of me that had a stake in what I felt about her. Either way, my dreams about my mother were all that remained of her for me, no photographs or letters or mementos of any kind. That was the way I'd wanted it. I wanted to forget her entirely if I could. The memories only brought me pain, and sleeplessness. I suddenly realized I was crying.

"Whaddya say, kiddo?"

Chapter Nine

NEXT MORNING, I lay in bed thinking about Sandy and how I might find her. I'd already looked for her name in the new phone book, without success. I'd seen her a few times over the past year in stores and restaurants, and my friends had seen her in various spots, so I had a working list of likely places to begin with. I figured her low profile might force me to be patient, but I was wrong.

I started looking for her at noon, and I found her in the third restaurant I checked, a place called More Than Eggs that specialized in omelets. There was a long counter with stools, scattered tables in the main part of the room, and booths against the windows and walls. It was a bright room of green vinyl and yellow wallpaper. When I saw her in a booth, I sat at the counter and ordered an omelet, turning sideways so I could keep an eye on her. I would have gone directly to her, but she was with someone, a man in a three-piece gray. They leaned toward each other across the table, hands meeting in the middle.

It was good just to see her, though I couldn't tell much about her from that distance. Her hair was shorter, and her clothes different. She laughed and fell back in her seat. This fellow wasn't good for her, smelled of too much money and politics. I'd figured she was going out, but I'd hoped to find her alone in the middle of the day. I wanted to avoid any unnecessary confrontations, though I wouldn't run away from a situation if it came to that. I studied him: a big man, short black hair neatly trimmed, fancy watch, thirty at least, too old for her, probably married or divorced.

The moment my intentions became focused, I could feel that force gathering behind my eyes. The distance and activity in the room didn't seem to matter. Slowly I unwrapped gray-suit's napkin and exposed his knife and fork and spoon. Sandy didn't notice, too busy talking, but gray-suit sure did. He interrupted her. She shook her head. They stared at his silverware for a few seconds as if they thought it might stand up and dance. They went back to talking.

I laughed. This could turn out to be more fun than I'd thought. I gave them a few minutes. Then I caused the salt shaker to move until it bumped into gray-suit's hand. He pulled his hand away and gawked at the shaker as if it were an iguana. Sandy stopped talking and was staring at him. He gestured at the shaker, seeming to introduce it to her. She shook her head and grinned. But gray-suit was insistent, getting both hands into the act for an assortment of gestures at the saltshaker. Sandy reached out and seized both his hands. I could almost hear what she was saying, telling him to cool it, to wait and see if it happened again. Both of them started looking around, and I had to turn my back. I didn't think she would recognize me from behind, not across that large room.

Their food came and they began to eat in silence, like two lovers who'd argued, neither wanting to give in. I knew I'd have to go for a little more. Suddenly gray-suit's omelet flopped in his plate like a fish just pulled from the water to the pier. He swallowed hard and laid his fork down. Sandy had seen it too. She made a small screeching sound and put her hands over her mouth. People at the nearest table had begun to stare at gray-suit and Sandy.

In the meantime, my omelet had come. I picked up my fork, took a bite. Carefully, I looked back at Sandy's booth. They were eating again, but timidly, prodding each bite to make sure it was dead. Then, gray-suit's omelet hopped straight up in the air. He slapped it down with his left hand and pinned it to the plate. He and Sandy looked at each other, wide-eyed. He grabbed a passing waitress and lifted his hand a little, cautiously, and nodded to the omelet. He was so excited, I could hear his voice over the crowd.

"There's something wrong with this omelet!"

The waitress mumbled a question.

"It won't hold still!"

The waitress put one hand on her hip and mumbled another question.

"How'm I supposed to eat it if I can't catch it?"

The waitress raised up straight, her tone of voice angry now. She walked abruptly away, face as straight as a pall-bearer's. Sandy and gray-suit were laughing hysterically. Things were not going the way I'd hoped. One more turn of the screw.

Gray-suit held his fork like a dagger, stalking what was left of his omelet with wild eyes. Sandy was still laughing, tears rolling down her face. Suddenly his expression changed. He dropped his fork and jammed the fingers of his right hand inside the collar of his shirt. His tie flew out from his throat like a flag in the wind. He was choking and he wasn't strong enough to stop it, not even with both hands. For a moment Sandy didn't know what to do and just stared at him, her face still flushed from laughing. I watched. It was easier than I'd thought. Much easier. My wish was the world's command. I wonder what my face might have looked like in that moment to anyone who noticed me. Gray-suit appeared to be wrestling with a pair of invisible hands around his neck. His face turned a dark red and spit flew from his mouth. Almost everyone in the restaurant turned toward him, and some came running over to help, but he waved them off, gasping, half-whispering that he was okay. He quickly undid his tie and pulled it off. Sandy looked frightened now. Gray-suit was still gasping a little, still rubbing his neck. He leaned towards her and said something.

That look of fear and worry on gray-suit's face was closer to what I'd been hoping for. I had to admit gray-suit not only had a sense of humor but he was pretty tough. He and Sandy were leaning towards each other over the table again, holding hands. It seemed to me that Sandy was trying to get him to leave, but he wanted to stay for a while, wanted to figure out what was happening. When his knife started spinning around on the table like a crazy compass needle, he pulled away from Sandy. The knife stopped, pointing straight at him. He slid cautiously from the booth like a man trying not to startle a snake. The point of the knife followed him. He backed away from the table.

He said something to Sandy, then turned, face drained of color, and ran through the maze of tables and through the heavy glass door. Out on the street he looked around nervously. He unwrapped three pieces of chewing gum and stuck them into his mouth. Sandy sat at the table in a kind of trance. She found her pocketbook, stood, and stared down at the knife on the table. She picked it up, turning it over and over. Finally she walked up to the cash register at the end of the counter three spaces from where I was sitting, her face fixed in a grimace. She was still beautiful, but she'd changed. A new idea behind her eyes, a new way of holding her mouth. Her face was heightened with a touch of make-up on her eyes and cheeks and lips. And her clothes, tight blue sweater and even tighter burgundy skirt.

"I don't have the check," Sandy said to the cashier, "but I can tell you what we had."

"I'm sorry," the cashier said, "but you'll have to get your check."

"Look, I'm in a hurry, the service here was rotten, and I have no intention of going back to that table."

Startled, the cashier stared at her for a second. "Well who was your waitress?"

"We didn't exchange names."

"Which was your table then?"

Sandy turned to point and looked straight into my eyes, her hand remaining in the air for a moment, even after the cashier had gone for the waitress. She took two steps toward me, then stopped, almost at attention, eyes unwavering. I breathed her perfume, which I'd never known her to wear. But it was her eyes that held me, blazing out of that thin mask of what she'd become.

"I need to see you," I said.

"Aren't you seeing me?"

"I want to talk to you."

The cashier returned with the check, and Sandy went back to the register. I waited behind her while she paid. Then she turned and started off as if I weren't there. I caught her at the door.

"Sandy, please, I have to see you."

She was slow to answer, but her eyes softened a little. "Okay. When?"

"Tonight."

She shook her head. "No. Not tonight. Tomorrow, for lunch, 12:30, at the Mayfair."

She turned and pushed through the door. She took gray-suit's arm and they walked away quickly, talking. There was an earnestness between them that made me feel sick inside.

THE ATMOSPHERE AT *The Sun* that afternoon didn't help. They were a club and I was a member who didn't belong. There was no use pretending otherwise. It wasn't that they deliberately excluded me. It was that silent communication between them that I didn't understand. It was the creepy feeling I had while I was there, my desire to get away as fast as I could, like a killer secretly passing among the victim's family. Fortunately, Frank was nowhere to be seen. If there was one person I did not want to deal with right now, it was Frank. But Phieffer was there, friendly as always, clapping me on the back, making small talk. As I drove away, I reminded myself that I couldn't continue working for *The Sun* much longer. I would have to find something else.

AT 12:25 SANDY was already waiting for me outside the smudged glass door of the Mayfair, arms crossed, glancing at her watch. The stony look in her eyes meant that there would be no closeness, no casual, lingering contact as we waited for a table, no snug placement of my hand at the small of her back to guide her through the door, no sense of really being together. I had felt this many times before with other girls, but never with Sandy. I would have to be patient.

The Mayfair was a hole-in-the-wall greasy spoon on a side street, one of the better places to go for a cheap but good hot meal. The room you entered from the outside was long and narrow, a small counter with cash register and candy just inside the door to the left. Down the long right side of the room were old booths covered in patched-up red naugahyde. Down the left side, there was a counter with stationary metal stools. Behind the counter, an ancient grill sizzled with steak sandwiches and onions. An old man who'd been cooking there for thirty years with passionate efficiency lowered a huge basket of frozen fries into the deep fryer. His smile was toothless, his beard white and scruffy, and his words incomprehensible. The waitresses, middle-aged, tough, cold until they got to know you, had learned through years of trial and error to communicate with the old man, and the Mayfair moved a mob of hungry lunchers in and out like a Toyota factory. I liked the Mayfair, but it was the worst place for meeting someone you wanted to talk to, and I had to wonder why Sandy chose it.

The entrance to the other room in the Mayfair was past the cash register to the left, with a green sign over the door that read, "The Green Room." You had to step down into a big, square, windowless, basement painted dark green and barely lit with small red-shaded lamps on the wall. The wooden chairs were stiff with wobbly legs and the tables were covered with green plastic tablecloths. I knew The Green Room was my best chance for quiet conversation under the circumstances.

The place was crowded as usual and we had to wait in line for a table. She stood in front of me with her back turned like any other stranger. She was going to make this as hard on me as she could. Finally, we were seated and a waitress that I knew well buzzed by, dropping two menus on the table. Sandy picked one up and appeared to be reading every word of it. I just stared at her, only her brown hair visible above the green menu. I had so much to say to her, but I didn't know how to get started.

Suddenly she slammed the menu down on the table. Her eyes blazed at me. "You're the one who did those things to us yesterday, aren't you?"

"Yes," I said. There was no point in lying. "I had to talk to you."

She furrowed her brow. "Why didn't you just come over and join us?"

"That didn't seem like an option."

"But humiliating us and scaring the hell out of us did?"

"I guess it was the wrong thing to do."

"You guess!" She gawked at me. "You don't have any idea what you've done to Sam's head, do you? He hasn't stopped talking about what happened since we left the restaurant. He thinks some kind of invisible demon was after him."

Maybe it was, I thought, but managed to say nothing.

"You think it's funny, don't you?"

"No," I said, "I just think you're exaggerating."

"How did you rig all that stuff up anyway?"

"I don't need to rig things up."

"You're telling me you did that on your own, with ESP or something?"

"Or something. Look, it was the first time I'd seen you in a long time. I guess I just wanted to show off."

"I don't believe you. Let's see you do something right now."

"Fine. What would you like me to do?"

She looked around the room. "See that man over there? The bald one? Make his tie fly up in his face."

I looked at the man. He was sitting alone at one of the small two-person tables, absent-mindedly eating as he read the paper in his left hand. Suddenly his tie slipped out of his coat and began to wag like a puppy's tail in his face. He set his fork down, grabbed the tie, which kept squirming in his hand, and stuffed it back inside his coat, never taking his eyes off the paper. He raised a forkful of food toward his mouth when the tie unfurled again like a tongue and slapped against his face. This time he freed both hands and forcefully tucked his tie back inside his coat. He glanced around the room to see if anyone had seen, and when his eyes caught mine he quickly went back to his paper.

I looked at Sandy.

"That's pretty unbelievable."

"I told you it was real."

"But why do you have to do something humiliating?"

"The tie was *your* idea, not mine."

"No, I just didn't think you'd do it."

"You mean you didn't think I *could* do it."

She just sat there for a moment with her arms crossed, staring at me like I'd stabbed someone with a knife. "Anyway, I don't care if you *do* have these powers. That's just something I've got to figure out. What I know for sure is that they're sort of like having big muscles. But it doesn't look good on you, Chuck. It makes you ugly."

"That was a nice little speech. You must've stayed up all night working on that one."

"You know, in one short year you've gone from a gentle boy to a genuine asshole. One year with Frank is all it took."

"It's strange that you think of me as a 'boy'."

"That's what you were, a lonely boy."

"Whatever I am now has nothing to do with Frank. So let's just leave him out of this."

"I don't think you could've become like this by yourself. Have you taken a good look at yourself lately?"

"Look who's talking. If you aren't a walking invitation for sex, then I ain't never seen one."

A waitress's hand came between us with two glasses of water. "You better be nice to this good-looking lady."

"Thank you," Sandy said.

"Hello Maggie. I'm being nice."

"Well, it didn't sound like you were. I think she looks beautiful." Sandy laughed.

"I think she's beautiful too. Maggie, this is Sandy."

"Sandra," Sandy said quickly, smiling.

Maggie looked from Sandy to me. "Right," she said. "Nice to meet you, honey." Then she stepped back and took out her pad and pen. Maggie wore the Mayfair uniform, a plain, light green dress with her name embroidered on her left breast pocket. Her hair was short, black and streaked with gray. She had a gaunt face with friendly buck teeth and gentle brown eyes that turned to ice if she got too busy or just fed up. Sandy and I ordered and Maggie hurried off.

"I guess she straightened *you* out," Sandy said.

"What does *she* know?"

"Look, this is the kind of stuff people are wearing now. There's nothing wrong with it."

"And what about your face? Do you have to wear all that junk on it?"

"I think you're jealous."

"Okay, so I'm jealous. I don't like the way men keep staring at you with their tongues hanging out."

"They don't do that. Besides, it's none of your business. We haven't been together for a year. Remember?"

"I remember."

"I've been wearing make-up since I was twelve. You just caught me in my low self-concept phase."

"If disguising your real face with make-up isn't low self-concept, then what is?"

"I don't want to discuss this with you. If you want to live in the world with other people, you have to pay attention to how you look. When I was with you, I was just with you. I wasn't working, I wasn't doing anything with my life."

"And now you are."

"Yes, I am."

"Like what?"

"I've got a good job as an administrative assistant. I'm finally using some of my education. I may even go back to school."

"I thought you were a scientist."

"That was a pipe dream."

"You call administrative assistant doing something with your life?"

"Yes, I do."

"It sounds pretty typical to me."

"I like typical."

"But you could have a better life than that."

"With you."

"Yeah, with me. You've seen what I can do."

"All I've seen are humiliating pranks."

"No. You know that's not what I mean. I've been trying to figure out what I could do with my abilities, and I think I've decided."

"What? Be a magician like Frank's father? Just what the world needs, another magician. I've got to give Frank credit where it's due. At least he has a realistic sense of his place in the world. He holds down a real job, you know? And keeps this magic stuff on the side like a hobby, where it belongs."

"Will you leave Frank out of this? I wasn't thinking magician, but it's similar. I could be a psychic."

"Like Uri Geller. He's a fake, you know. I've been reading about him."

"Maybe he is. But I'm not. Scientists would want to study my powers and write books about it. I could make a lot of money Sandy, and we could travel. We could do anything we want."

"You're dreaming Chuck. It could never happen."

"No. You're wrong. *This* could happen. My powers are real."

"Even if it could happen, I don't want any part of it. It's not the kind of life I want."

"What *do* you want?"

"I want to be normal. I want to live a long, dull, normal life."

"You mean a middle-class life."

"Yes, what's wrong with that?"

"Nothing, if you don't have any choice. I can't believe you'd choose that over what I can offer you."

"Believe," she said, laughing.

Maggie reached between us with our two ice teas and a green plastic basket containing hot rolls. We just stared at each other while Maggie tended to her business, Sandy with that look of amusement, in control. Maggie finished, raised up and looked back and forth between the two of us, shrugged her shoulders and walked off.

When she was out of the way, I leaned forward. "Are you sleeping with him?"

"With whom?"

"You know, the omelet-man in the three-piece gray."

"That's none of your business."

"I think it is."

"I know you do. That's what's so funny. But I don't really mind telling you in this case. I haven't slept with him yet, but I might. I like Sam a lot."

"Do you sleep with everybody you like?"

Maggie returned with two plates of steaming hot food. She set them down, then raised up with her arms folded across her chest. "Well," she said, looking at Sandy, "*Do* you?"

Sandy glanced up at Maggie and blushed. Then she gave me a wide-eyed "help me" look.

"Come on Maggie. Give us a break."

Maggie waggled her eyebrows at me. Then she pranced away.

"That's one strange lady," Sandy said.

I leaned toward her. "Well do you?"

She leaned forward too, speaking softly and slowly, her face filled with that cool amusement. "I sleep with whomever I choose."

"So it's 'whomever' now. You've even changed the way you talk."

"I have to do it the right way at work, so I try to speak it the right way. You know, I think you expected me to remain that sad, dumpy little pushover forever, just for you."

"Is that really the way you see it?"

"That's the way it *was*. And I admit it, I was in love with you, partly because you were the same as me, a drop-out with nothing to do. I can't go back to that, Chuck, not even for you."

"Maybe I've changed too. Maybe I don't want to go back to that either."

"You've changed alright, but in a bad way. You've got that 'I dare you' look in your eyes just like those muscle men when they come into a bar. And that's the only thing different about you. You wear the same clothes, you live in the same dump, you have the same stupid, dead-end job. Jesus, Chuck, you couldn't pay the rent on my apartment, much less utilities, food, clothes, insurance." She counted them out on her fingers. "I don't want to be poor any more."

"Okay, I can understand that. I'll do it your way. I'll find a good job. I figure my powers can help me in anything I do."

"Who would hire you, Chuck? You haven't even graduated from high school."

I shook my head and took a deep breath.

"Look," she said, "I didn't come here to put you down."

"You could've fooled me."

"It's just that we're not the same any more. Maybe we never were. You should do what you want to do. But you need to find a girl who wants to share that kind of life with you. I'm just not she. I'm tired of being an outsider. I've been pulling that routine for years and it just wears you out. You were my last rebellion, Chuck. You were my way of hurting my parents. When you flipped out, that was the end of my rebel days. Now my parents and I are getting along better than we ever have. That's another thing I don't want to spoil."

"What was your problem with them in the first place?"

"A man. One they didn't approve of. Boy were they ever right about him. They wouldn't approve of you either, Chuck. That's why I stayed clear of them in those days."

"And what about the omelet-man? Do they approve of him?"

"Yes, they like Sam a lot. Why shouldn't they? He's a respected young lawyer with a good future. And he's a nice guy."

I could feel that everything I wanted to say was designed to hurt her feelings, to get back at her, to prolong the argument. And that wasn't going to work. It wasn't going to make her see that we should be together. I would have to think of something else. Both of us ate quietly for a while.

She put her fork down and looked at me.

"There's something I want to ask you."

"Go ahead."

"Why did you wait so long? If you felt so strongly about me, why didn't you call?"

"You told me not to."

"You thought I really meant that? As close as we were, I find that hard to believe."

"Sandy, I thought Frank was offering me a chance at something really amazing. As it turned out, I was right. I just didn't realize how long it would take. I wanted to come back to you with something to offer."

"You remember the night we met, at that little bar?" she said. "That's the Chuck I fell in love with. I hate all this power stuff and what it's doing to you."

"I've just got something extra now, that's all. I'm still the same guy."

"Well I wish I could see him. When I first saw you yesterday, I had such a strong feeling, I wanted to take you in my arms. Then I saw that different look in your eyes and I realized you'd played those mean tricks on Sam, and what was left of my old feelings for you just disappeared right then. If you'd called me any time in those first six months I'm almost sure we'd be together right now. I had it bad for you Chuck. It was not an easy time for me."

"Does six months really make that much difference?"

"In this case it does. Once I got past a certain point, I just stopped thinking about you. Then it was easy. I really like my new life."

"I can't just give up on us like this, Sandy."

She glanced at her watch, then dropped her napkin on the table. "I've got to get back to work."

"You didn't eat much."

"I had enough."

"Can I call you?"

"I'd rather you didn't. This time I mean it."

She stood up and picked up her check.

"Let me pay." I reached for it.

"No," she said, pulling it away. "Dutch treat." She stood for a moment to study me. I didn't know what to do with myself, where to put my hands, whether to return her gaze. "You want to know something?" she said, "I still don't believe it. I saw it with my own eyes, but I still think there's something fishy about this power of yours.

Worse than fishy, Chuck. Something silly about it. You know what I mean?" She grabbed her pocketbook and turned away.

As she walked out almost every man in the room took a good look at her. It was the way she moved, that honest, agile stride of hers. And the clothes she wore: another tight skirt and sweater, and I had to admit I couldn't take my eyes off her either. It didn't make my life any easier to want to punch out every guy that stared at her. There were too many, unless I was going to use my powers to wage war against every straight man in town. As she stood in the short line waiting to pay, I was tempted to pull her skirt right over her head. That might just teach her something. The urge became so strong I had to turn around and stare at the table in front of me. Otherwise, I was going to do it, and that would be the end for sure.

"Are you finished?" Maggie asked.

"Yeah, we're finished."

Maggie flopped down in Sandy's chair and ran her hand through her hair. "I'm bushed."

"Yeah," I said, glancing at her, "you do look tired. Have some lunch. We got plenty."

Maggie pointed at Sandy's plate: a mound of lima beans, macaroni and cheese, a fried flounder curling up. "I never eat this shit. I spend too much time looking at it. You know what I mean?"

I nodded.

"Ain't that the same girl you used to hang around with?"

"Yeah, that's the one."

"Damn, that is one fine looking piece."

"Maggie . . ."

"Now wait a minute," she said, pointing with her thumb, "I'm just saying what those two guys over there are thinking." She took stock of me. "It didn't go so hot between you two, did it?"

"You interrupting us all the time didn't help none either. What's wrong with you today?"

"I was just doing my job. Besides, I made her laugh a couple times, didn't I? You got to give a girl like that a lot of laughs. She don't want to mope around all the time."

"I'll keep that in mind. She's just testing me, that's all."

"Are you gonna pass?"

"She's got me stumped right now, but I'll work it out."

"Well, if you need any consultation, I'm available, and the price is right." Her face sank lower over that mound of lima beans.

"If you're not careful," I said, "you're gonna fall right in that plate."

"That's okay honey, I could use a good facial anyway."

I laughed. "Maggie, they should all be like you."

"If they were all like me, Chuck, there would be no more children."

I laughed again. "That's not true. Just lots of ugly children."

She threw her head back and guffawed. "You *are* mean today."

"No, really, Maggie, you're not bad looking."

"You really think so?"

"Yeah, you're a lot worse than that."

Maggie laughed so hard the tears ran down her cheeks. I didn't think I was that funny. What does it mean when someone laughs so hard at jokes that aren't funny? "Now see what I mean about laughing?" she said between gasps, "I feel better already."

I left her a big tip and she got up and started clearing off the table. As I waited at the cash register for my change, I realized that I had strong feelings about Maggie, though I'd never seen her outside of these rooms. I looked back into The Green Room where she was cleaning off another table. Her face was straight now, deep in thought. She did not look happy. I wanted to do something really nice for her sometime. Something that would make her feel good.

But first I had to get things squared away with Sandy. The Omelet-Man would have to go.

"Sit down," Frank said, looking up from his desk.

I sat down. Frank put his hands behind his head, leaning back with his feet on the desk, looking at me down the length of his body.

"You said you wanted to talk to me," I said.

"Oh, yeah." Frank rubbed the stubble on his face. "I did, didn't I?"

"Jesus Frank, you look pretty strung out."

"Yeah, I guess I do. Usual state of affairs." He grinned and yawned at the same time. "I been pretty busy."

"That's good Frank. Listen, I don't mean to rush you . . ."

"I want you to come by my house tonight."

I grimaced. "I can't Frank. I've got plans."

"Cancel them."

"Just like that."

"I wouldn't ask you if it wasn't important."

"Frank, I understand how you feel. But you've got to let me go my own way now. You've got to let all these other people go too."

Frank laughed and shook his head. "I'm not holding anybody here against their will. But you don't really know enough yet to understand what's going on. Let's talk about this later, around 7:30."

I hated this, but what could I say? I figured I owed Frank at least this much. One last visit to the house where I'd seen and experienced so many strange things, where I'd learned about the power.

I bolted down to my car. I'd still have time to get started on my Omelet-Man project, if I could make quick work of the route.

IT WOULD HAVE been easy to follow Sandy, but if she spotted me it would make her uncomfortable, maybe even scared. I never wanted her to be afraid of me. I finally managed to reach Sharon, one of her old roommates who had her address and phone number. She hadn't seen Sandy for a while, but said that she talked about me a lot after we'd split up. She was sure that Sandy wanted to hear from me.

The Omelet-Man wasn't hard to locate either. After all, a young lawyer wants to be easy to find. Samuel T. Burnett, attorney at law, with a downtown office and a condo on Shoreline Drive.

Now if I could just get Frank out of my way, maybe I could do something about this situation. I would have to pry the Omelet-Man out of her life and ease myself back into it.

WHEN I GOT to Frank's, the front door was open. I strolled through the dimly lit house and out the back door into the yard where Frank and his mother were sitting in quiet conversation, looking up at the night sky. There was an empty chair between them, and a table and a cooler in front. Each of them held a bottle of beer and another was on the table, flecks of ice sliding down the glass. Beer just didn't seem like the right thing for Lyuba to be drinking.

I stopped in front of Lyuba and met her friendly but curious gaze straight on. She was an amazing looking woman in her long blue dress, her long straight black hair turning gray, dark skin and dark eyes. Striking—her face, her hands. Her dress was slightly crumpled, and loose hairs floated about her head as if she were somehow beyond the rituals of hygiene and kept them up half-heartedly as a matter of necessity only. I couldn't resist bowing to her.

She smiled.

"Have a seat," Frank said.

I sat down and took a long drink from the beer I knew was meant for me. I looked at Frank. "I see you brought out the heavy artillery tonight."

Frank laughed.

Lyuba was smiling, but the look in her eyes seemed to come from a great distance. "Young man . . ."

"Chuck's the name."

"Very well, Chuck. The heavy artillery, as you put it, is not a person, or a thing."

I looked back and forth at the two of them. "Okay. You've got me surrounded. Say what you've got to say and let's get this thing over with."

"We just want you to calm down." She reached out to touch my forearm, a zing of tension running up my arm and into my chest. "Take things a little more slowly for a while."

"Look, I've taken too much time as it is. The things I really want from life are getting away from me. I've got to act now while there's still time."

She smiled again, and her face seemed to grow younger. It would be impossible to guess her age.

"If you really knew what you wanted, that would be fine. You think you want this young woman, Sandra. Think, in fact, that you must have her or you can't go on living. But you don't know what you want. You've forgotten what you really want. Sandra isn't it, not in the way you think she is."

"I see," I said. "You people are really amazing. You think you know everything, right down to what I'm thinking, right down to what I want. What I really want is to get as far away from the two of you as I can."

I took a long drink and wiped my mouth on the sleeve of my sweatshirt. I started to stand, but something pulled me back into the chair. I tried again, but I couldn't pull myself away. Then I saw them, two bands of light around my chest, strapping me to the chair. I grabbed at them, but my hands went through them like air, yet they held me in place.

"We haven't finished talking," Frank said.

I became frantic. I tried to muscle the chair away from my body. I twisted and lunged, wrestling the chair as if it were alive. I fell on my side, face pressing into the freshly cut grass. The chair righted itself somehow and I found myself seated before them, their eyes calm, maybe the slightest glint of amusement. If only I could get my hands on them.

"Chuck," she said, "there's a lot more you need to find out about yourself before you start taking *any* course of action. You are not a new member of our group. You've been one of us for thousands of years."

"That doesn't make any sense."

"I know it doesn't. The things you think are important aren't so important. I know that sounds arrogant, but it's not. It's the truth. Will you let me tell you some other things that are true?"

I took a deep breath and let it out. "Be my guest."

"Good decision," she said. Her eyes met Frank's for a second, then she sat back in her chair. "Frank and I have deflected your momentum. For some reason you continue to fight it. The light that's in you is the same as the light that's in me. It's not that we are similar, we are the same being talking to itself. We are not separate from each other, we are the same. This is the reality, Chuck."

"That's just . . . I don't know . . . creepy. Okay? I'm grateful for what you've given me. But I'm not interested in your religion. I've got my own life to live."

Frank had pulled out a cigarette, but didn't light it. "When you thought I had something you wanted, you believed everything I told you. Now all of a sudden you don't believe a word we say."

"Because it's stupid hocus pocus."

"If the powers are real, then what we're saying must be true. What could make more sense?"

"It's no use," Lyuba said to Frank. "The momentum of the old way is still running its course inside him." She turned to me. "You don't have any idea what's happening to you because you're still fighting it instead of listening to it. You can't tell the power what to do. The power chooses you and uses you. Why do you think you have these recurring dreams? That's one of the ways we're connected to the power and to each other. There's too much work to be done for you to continue this personal indulgence. The lineage extends itself across all time and space, and you're part of it, whether you like it or not, and you've got to help us find the others."

"Convert the others . . . is what you mean. Right?"

"Inform them," she said. "It's only a matter of degree. We're all a part of this thing. Frank and I are just trying to pass on the information, to people who are ready for it. Sometimes we make a mistake."

The bands of light around my chest faded away, and I stood up.

Frank leaned forward to grab me by the arm, but Lyuba put her hand on his shoulder. "Let him go," she said. "It would be foolish to give him more at this stage."

I stood there looking at them for a minute. "You know, you two should see yourselves. A couple of comic strip characters or something. A butch Bela Lugosi and a sexy wicked witch of the north. Control freaks, if you ask me. I've been through the religion thing. God is love, so jump when we say jump, all that crap. Let's all hold hands and sing 'Amazing Grace'. You've just changed the terms and the titles. Not everybody wants this stuff. And that's the real truth."

Neither one of them moved or said a word, just kept looking at me. I saluted them each in turn, then walked across the lawn with my hands in my pockets. I strolled through the house stopping to look at some of those old photos of magicians and their families.

Through the open back door I could see the two of them still sitting there, barely visible in the light from neighboring houses. Suddenly their voices popped into my head as if I were still sitting between them.

"I told you he was stubborn," Frank's voice said in my left ear.

"It doesn't matter," the woman's voice said in my right ear.

And then there was silence again. I laughed out loud, hoping they could hear. The power was showing more of itself to me every day. Frank and Lyuba could not have been more wrong, I knew myself better than ever before. Knew, more certainly than ever, what it was that I wanted.

Chapter Ten

WHEN I GOT home, the night was cool and clear, so I took a walk. I glanced into the bars and beer joints, but wasn't really interested in drinking. I felt good that night, proud of the way I'd stood up to Frank and Lyuba.

There were only a few people on the street. Barflies trying not to look like they'd had too much. Occasionally a group of young men near my own age. Almost no women. There'd been a time when I was hesitant to go out on these particular streets at night, though I often did it anyway out of loneliness or some strange notion of self-discipline. But now I felt invulnerable. There was no gang, no muscle-bound mugger that could lay a hand on me. People seemed to sense my confidence and stayed away.

My mind wandered. I dreamed of clearing up the trouble with Sandy, of getting married, of earning the wealth and fame that I deserved. I dreamed of the children Sandy and I would have that we could bring up under the protection of the power—not some phony religion. My desires were simple and good, it seemed to me.

But first I would have to do something about Sam the Omelet-Man. I'd already put a good scare into him. It shouldn't be hard to push the guy a little farther.

I went home and headed straight for bed, wanting to get a good night's rest. Tomorrow I would begin. It had been many years since I'd felt this kind of possibility, excitement, and fear.

I WOKE UP groggy in the hospital waiting room—the hospital where my mother lay dying slowly. My father and brothers had gone home hours ago. The room was full of imitation leather chairs and couches, dimly lit by the square of light from the door's window and the red glow of the Coke machine in the far corner. I could have stayed in a more comfortable room with a bed, but I wanted to be close to my mother,

I took a few minutes to clear my head, to make sure I was alert. For the last month, I'd gathered the knowledge I needed for this night. Of the several methods that had come to my attention, I felt I'd selected the easiest, the most efficient. I checked my watch: 2:05. I unrolled my jacket, which I'd been using as a pillow, and put it on. Except for a low, barely audible hum of electricity, the building was silent. Somewhere, maybe on another floor, there were problems and people were busy trying to solve them. But here, everything was still.

I got up and entered the hall of the ward, milk-white walls, heavy wooden doors to the rooms all closed. The nurse wasn't at her station. From trial runs on previous nights, I knew she probably wouldn't be. I stepped behind the counter, into the room where the medicines were kept and scanned the shelves until I saw what I was looking for: several rows of 30 cc vials of Potassium Chloride. I took one vial from the back of the shelf and was out of the nursing station within fifteen seconds of entering. I forced a deep breath into my lungs, put my hands in my pockets and made myself stroll up the hall. If anyone saw me, wanted to know what I was doing, I'd say I was just restless, stretching my legs.

I still couldn't hear any voices or the sound of the nurse's steps on the tile floor. I opened the door to the supply room and slipped in, closing it quietly behind me. The walls had shelves from ceiling to floor stocked with nursing supplies. There was a supply cart in the middle of the room. I'd followed Sheila, one of my mother's young nurses, into this room one day, so I knew the syringes were kept in the near corner to the right. It took me a moment to find what I wanted, a box of 35 cc syringes, each sealed individually in a clear plastic package. I put one in my pocket, eased back into the hall and returned to the couch in the waiting room. I sat there for a few minutes trying to calm myself. The easy part was done. Now came the hard part. I stared at the yellow label on the vial of Potassium Chloride: Sterile. Nonpyrogenic.

MY MOTHER'S ROOM was not entirely dark. There was the glow of a small night light in a baseboard outlet, and the pale light of the night sky through the partially open curtain of her window. I stood beside the bed and looked at her. She was asleep, the sheet pulled up snug across her chest and under her arms, head fallen slightly to the left, the outline of her body seemingly frail under the sheet, face and hands thick and puffy, left arm swollen all the way up. The IV was inserted in a vein on the right side of her neck. A large plastic bag of fluid hung from a metal stand.

I sat down in a chair under the window and took a slow, deep breath to calm myself. I would never have believed this was my mother if I'd not witnessed the process that brought her to this point, the operations, the chemotherapy. Sometimes I felt that this really wasn't my mother, that some mistake had been made. I sat there for a long time—very still and relaxed. I wasn't sure if I would ever move again.

Her breath stopped and started. She raised her head a little, blinking her eyes.

"Who is that? Charles?"

"Yes."

"Why aren't you home?"

"I wanted to stay here with you."

"All the others went home?"

"Yes."

"You should be home too. You need your sleep."

"I'm okay."

She just kept looking at me. She lifted her head and moved it from side to side as if she were trying to make something out in the complicated light. The medication was always making her see things that weren't there.

"Where'd you get that paper crown?"

I put my hand on top of my head.

"It looks just like the one you wore in your sixth grade play, and it didn't fit right and kept falling off while you were making your important decrees. Do you remember?"

"I remember."

"You were a beautiful king."

"I wish I was a real king."

"Only children can be kings and queens. There aren't any real ones."

"You're a real queen to me," I said, unable to stop myself, glad she couldn't see me blushing in the dim light.

She laughed softly and suppressed a cough. "Sometimes I actually feel that you don't hate me."

I shook my head. "You know I don't hate you, Mother."

"I know. But there's always something wrong, a distance. I can feel it. Why is that?"

"I don't know. Maybe I . . . It's always been hard for me to be with you."

"No, it wasn't always like that. Not when you were little."

"I remember. But that was a long time ago."

"Not so long ago."

"I was a momma's boy if ever there was one."

"Maybe we can have a truce now. We can be at peace."

"Yeah. We can be at peace."

She turned her head and stared up at the ceiling. I leaned back to be more in the shadow and took out the syringe and the vial of Potassium Chloride. I tore the syringe out of the plastic wrapper, removed the long plastic cap that covered the needle, then flipped off the yellow top of the vial. I'd seen the nurses do this a thousand times. I turned the vial upside down and inserted the needle through the rubber seal, withdrew the solution into the syringe. My hands were shaking, and there was resistance, as if the vial was trying to suck the liquid back, but most of it came out. There was a tiny release of air when I pulled the needle back through the rubber seal. I put the vial and its yellow top back into my pocket along with the plastic wrapper and ran a couple of drops out of the needle because the nurses always did that.

"Now that your brothers aren't around, I can ask you," my mother said, turning her head back to face me. "Are you going out with Sarah?"

"No. I'm not going out with anyone."

"I thought you liked her."

"I do like her, but it's not that simple. Maybe I'll ask her out later. Not now, not for a while."

"She's a beautiful girl."

"Yeah. She's beautiful."

"You were always the shy one."

"I guess so."

"You know, I love your brothers. They're becoming good strong men like your father. But you've always been special to me. Did you know that?"

"You shouldn't be saying things like that."

"I know. I don't know why I'm talking on like this. I can trust you not to repeat any of this, can't I? It just feels good to say what you think." She smiled at me. "You're the strange one, the smart one. You can be anything you want. When I get out of this place, I'll help you with your diving. That's a good discipline to start from. Everybody needs at least one discipline in their life. You know what I mean?"

"Mother, why do you keep lying to yourself?"

She turned her face away from me and was silent for a minute. Then she turned toward me again.

"I'm not lying to myself," she said. "I'm lying to you. I know I'm dying. I'm not a fool."

"It's alright Mother . . ."

"Of course it's alright. Like most things there's nothing to be done about it. I've been thinking about it a lot Charles, and I've decided that dying is okay. You know, there's a part of me that's not sick at all, that's doing just fine. That may sound crazy, but I know it's true. The closer I get to dying the less I have to worry about. I'm pretty much down to nothing now Charles. There's a part of me that's already free, and that feels good. Except that I still worry about you. You're the only thing."

"I'm doing fine."

"You're not ready to be alone in the world like the others. Your brothers, they have the church and your father. They'll be salesmen just like him. They'll do fine. But you're different. You don't have the foggiest idea what's going on or where you're headed, and it worries me."

"I'll be alright too, Mother."

"Probably so."

I stood up and walked towards her. She saw the syringe in my hand and smiled.

"Are you playing nurse tonight?"

"Yes, I'm your nurse for the night."

I'd hoped to do all of this while she was still asleep. But maybe this was better after all. Better to see her eyes, to talk to her, to be clear about what I was doing. I found the injection port on the IV tube. She turned her head to watch. She showed no concern but wrinkled her brow out of curiosity. Close to her now I could see her eyes inside of those puffy eyelids, that clear, direct, beautiful look of hers still there, breaking through the sedatives. I stroked the side of her face and neck.

"You know," she said, "I believe you really do love me."

"Yes, I do."

I removed the cap from the port, squeezed the tube off above it, and inserted the needle. I forced the solution in with the heel of my right hand and removed the needle. I reached up and increased the flow from the IV bag, flushing the tube into her blood stream. I reset the drip.

"What are you doing?" she asked.

I just looked into those quizzical eyes. My lips were trembling, I couldn't make them stop. I wanted to say something, but there were no words for what I was doing, for what I was feeling.

Suddenly her eyes widened and she looked away from me to the ceiling. Her body jerked. "Oh no," she said. "Oh God . . ." Her eyes rolled back into her head. Her body convulsed once, then again, then a third time, then relaxed into one long exhalation. She was still now. I straightened the sheet up around her. I closed her eyes and made her look just as she had looked when I'd walked into the room. I stood beside the bed for a moment and stroked her arm. I knew the nurse was not due to bring the pain-killers for another hour. I closed my eyes and breathed deeply, trying to relax the trembling out of my body. If someone were to see me, I'd have to be calm.

I turned around to leave and saw someone, a woman, standing in the darkness near the doorway. A sharp pang of anxiety tightened my stomach. Had she seen it all? I took a step closer. There was no expression in her eyes, no judgement, no outrage. She was simply observing me. It was Lyuba.

I WOKE UP and sat up on the side of my bed. It felt like the pounding of my heart was shaking the whole room. Sometimes when I dreamed about her, my mother, it was hard for me to find the point of present reality to return to. Was I still inside the dream? I felt a sickness unlike anything I'd ever known. Lyuba was in my dream. She'd been as real as myself, as my mother, if anything is real in a dream. Was any dream I had now only a dream? I'd felt the heat from her body as I'd slid past her in the room's foyer. Maybe she'd been there the first time, when it really happened. Maybe she'd known about it all along. I held my face in my hands and cried. I'd killed my own mother, and Lyuba saw me do it.

I returned in my memory to that night in the hospital. Lyuba stepped towards me, shrinking the mouth of the foyer as I tried to get by, her face only inches from my own. I stopped and tried to read her eyes. Her face was so calm I wanted to touch it to see if it wasn't stone. Something was there, not amusement as I'd expected, not disgust or hatred, no judgment of any kind, only this looking into me as if I were a great room to be explored. But there was something more, and I was suddenly afraid, and I backed away from her toward the door. But she wasn't pursuing me. She turned and walked toward my mother. I wanted to see what she was doing, but I had to get out of there.

I managed to make it back to the waiting room without being seen. I put the syringe and the vial in a McDonald's paper bag along with some other trash and stuck it in the trashcan. I pretended to sleep on the couch. No one came for me that night. When my father walked into the room the next morning and put his hand on my shoulder, I sat up yawning, screwing up my face. I knew I looked like hell and said, "I had a terrible dream."

That day I was free to show all my emotions, and I broke down completely. No foul play was suspected in a case like this, since she was near the end anyway. No autopsy was done, at the request of the family. I got away with it free and clear. It was several weeks before I had, with medication, a normal night's sleep. Six months later, I drove my beat-up Beetle out of town after school and just kept on going. But for several years it was a rare night that I didn't return to that hospital room in my dreams. I remembered now, it was only after I'd started having the spider dreams that the dreams about my mother had faded away. I felt that Frank and Lyuba were consuming me entirely. There was nothing left that was only mine, not even my dreams—not even my memories. I knew why Lyuba had frightened me so much. She'd been there all along, though I'd never been able to see her before. She'd always been with me, making me feel different and estranged from the world around me. That look in her eyes . . . If I'd stood before her for another instant, she would've embraced me. I was certain she was going to take me into her arms.

If only I could go to Sandy now. The pain of wanting her, needing her, was driving me insane.

AFTER BREAKFAST I drove downtown and parked across the street from the Omelet-Man's office building, rode the elevator to the eighth floor, studying my curved, elongated image in the metal door. I was wearing my only suit, a cheap but not bad-looking brown coat and pants with dark brown socks and tan shoes, plain brown tie and ivory shirt. I'd spent almost every cent I had on it when I first came to town, thinking it would help me get a job, and wore it a few times when I was filling out applications. Then Frank hired me, and I'd never seen Frank in a suit.

When I found the office of Burnett, Laughlin and Lyle, a pretty brunette glanced up at me through the glass door and went back to her typing. I sat in a hall chair next to the elevator, opened up my newspaper and began to read.

Just before nine o'clock Sam the Omelet-Man emerged from the elevator wearing a sharp, three piece gray suit with a briefcase dangling from his left hand. He was pre-occupied and didn't notice me. The office door was at the end of the hall and I had a clear view over the top of my paper.

The Omelet-Man took hold of the handle and pulled, but the door didn't open. The secretary looked up at him and smiled. Sam was a big man, well over six feet and 200 pounds, and he glared at the door like a man who wasn't accustomed to resistance. He leaned back and put a more serious effort into it, but still the door wouldn't budge. The secretary's smile dwindled into puzzlement. The Omelet-Man set his briefcase down on the floor and put both hands on the handle, pulling and jerking with all of his weight. But it was like trying to pull a wall down with nothing but a doorknob. Sam was breathing heavily now, his face bright red. He knocked on the glass and signaled to his secretary who got up from her desk and gave the door a little shove. It swung open smoothly, then eased shut again. Sam stared at the door and shook his head. The secretary shrugged her shoulders from her side of the glass. He took the handle, but again the door wouldn't open.

"Goddamnit," he said.

The secretary pushed the door open with her left hand. "I'll hold it for you Mr. Burnett."

"Let's get somebody in here to fix this thing." He leaned over to pick up his briefcase. But it wouldn't move. He bent his knees and used his legs to lift, but the briefcase appeared to be nailed to the floor, the grip stretched almost to breaking.

"I'll get it for you," she said and stepped out into the hall. She picked up the briefcase and opened the door and held it for him.

"What the hell is going on here?" he said.

"I don't know. What did you eat for breakfast?"

"Very funny," he said, pausing to look at something on her desk as the door swung closed behind them.

Suddenly he turned, glaring down the hall through the glass door. I held the newspaper high. I was certain Sam had seen no more than part of my face before disappearing into his office.

Not since I was a small boy had I experienced such a feeling: pure glee. "This is going to be fun," I thought. I headed for the elevator.

I CHANGED INTO jeans and a T-shirt, flopped down in a used lounge chair I'd bought when my income had gone up, and began to print, bearing down hard, making the letters thick and clear:

RULES FOR SURVIVAL

1. STOP SEEING SANDY

2. TELL HER THERE'S ANOTHER WOMAN

*3. TELL HER NOTHING ABOUT THIS NOTE OR WHAT HAS
    HAPPENED*

4. FOLLOW THESE RULES, OR ELSE . . .

I folded the paper, sealed it in an envelope and addressed it. I took out a ten dollar bill and attached it to the envelope with a paper clip.

At 11:00, I returned downtown and found a parking place near Sam's building. Then I walked a block and a half and stepped into Mr. B's Midnight Tavern. It was a dark place with a dark wooden bar that cracked and creaked when you leaned on it, old wooden stools that spun around, and a scattering of wooden tables and chairs. Mr. B was a vigorous seventy years old, tall, almost skeletally thin, bald as a fist with a gray scraggly beard he claimed was sexy.

"Well, if it isn't Chuckles," said Mr. B, his gray eyes flashing like the street in the mirror behind him. He'd called me "Chuckles" since a silly, drunken night I'd spent in the bar two years ago.

"How're you doing Mr. B?"

"Good as gold. What'll you have?"

"Nothing right now. I've got to go to work in a while."

"Well damn son, this is a bar ain't it? What're you doing in here this time of the day?"

"I always wondered why you opened up so early."

"Hell, ain't got nothing better to do. Besides, the sad truth is . . . some people need a drink this time of the day. It's kind of a special service I provide."

Mr. B hired a couple of college kids who came in around 4:30 and helped him run the bar till closing.

"I came in to have a word with Ted," I said, settling down on a stool beside another old gentleman. "How's life treating you Ted?"

"Never better," he said, clearing his throat, nursing his first glass of whiskey for the day. He'd drink four or five of those before the day was over, sipping on them slowly. He'd have been on the streets and dead years ago if Mr. B hadn't taken him in. Mr. B lived in the rooms above the bar. When Ted got laid off, he was sixty years old with practically nothing saved up and no place to go. His wife went on to California to live with her younger sister. Mr. B gave Ted a room upstairs and a little spending money in exchange for a few hours work every day, cleaning up and running errands. They'd been together for years.

"I'd be kind of interested to know what business you got with old Ted here." Mr. B slid his bartender's stool over so he could hear better.

"Me too," Ted said, leaning toward me, grinning. A distinguished looking man, stouter than Mr. B., clean shaven with a few strands of gray hair swept across the top of his head, he owned three or four old suits which he kept in perfect repair. Unless he was working, you always found him in one of those suits: shirt, tie, suspenders, spit-shined shoes, but I had never seen him in his coat.

I explained what I wanted Ted to do.

"Sounds like an easy ten bucks to me," Ted said.

"And it would really mean a lot to me. I'd give you more if I could afford it."

"Nah, that's plenty. I'll be glad to do it."

"Say," said Mr. B, "you're not going to get Ted in trouble are you?"

"No way. I just want to get this note to the guy without him knowing where it came from. That's all."

"What about letting us have a look at that note." Mr. B placed his hand over the envelope on the bar between them.

"Well, it's already sealed. Besides, it's personal."

"Ted, I think there's something fishy about all this," Said Mr. B. "But I reckon you ought to help the boy out."

Ted slid off his stool and headed toward a dark corner of the room. "This job calls for full gear," he said, pulling a coat down from a hook on the wall. He put it on, straightened out the lapel and buttoned the middle button. "Reporting for duty sir." He came to attention and saluted.

IT WAS TEN minutes past noon before Sam emerged from the huge, glass double doors of his building. His coat was unbuttoned. He checked his watch, then stepped down to the sidewalk and strode off briskly.

He's in a mighty big hurry to get somewhere, I thought. Probably meeting Sandy for lunch.

"That's your cue," I said, giving Ted a pat on the shoulder. We got out of the car. "Remember, deliver the note to his secretary and come straight out."

"Gotcha." Ted crossed the street and went into Sam's building.

I fed the parking meter another quarter and followed Sam at a safe distance on the other side of the street. But Sam moved with a purpose and I was beginning to lose sight of him.

Got to slow him down, I thought, got to get him under control.

Sam tripped and slammed against a man walking in the opposite direction. The man took two steps back, knees buckling, and almost went down. He had long black hair, mustache and a beard, black leather boots, pants and vest with silver studs. He was pissed off, right hand balled up in a fist. Sam was apologizing, explaining with shrugs of the shoulders and uplifted palms. The other man relaxed, shook his head without saying anything and walked on. For a few seconds Sam stared back at the sidewalk where he'd been walking, then headed off again, a little slower this time.

By now I had come up even with Sam on the other side of the street. I felt a little like a shepherd dog working a wayward sheep. I was amazed at the suppleness and accuracy of this power, this energy, light, force . . . whatever it was. It uncoiled from me like a snake's tongue and moved unnoticed through crowds of people and automobile traffic and attached itself to the object of my intention: Sam.

Sam tripped again, but less wildly this time. He stopped, did a 360 turn scanning the sidewalk, leaned over and ran his hands up and down his calves and shins. He suddenly stood up, a look of recognition settling across his broad, handsome face. I figured Sam would begin to connect his problem with the strange occurrences in the restaurant, and with the door episode. I wondered if Sandy had told Sam anything about me, my powers. I thought not. Not yet anyway.

Sam gave everybody around him a good look and moved more cautiously now, like a man being stalked by an assassin, knees slightly bent, hands held in readiness instead of stuffed into pockets. He crouched nervously when he crossed the street, feeling himself more exposed, more vulnerable to whatever was after him. When he stepped onto the curb, a large, metal trash container toppled over in front of him. Sam lunged backwards into the street and landed on all fours as if someone had taken a shot at him.

A small crowd gathered around the container, trying to figure out what had happened. Another young executive type helped Sam to his feet. Sam looked relieved to find someone he knew. He couldn't stop talking, shaking his head, gesturing back down the street where he'd been walking. He leaned over slightly and pulled at the knees of his pants, which were ruined. The other guy nodded and spoke for a few seconds. Then the two of them started walking together. After a few steps, Sam tripped and caught himself against the wall of a building. He resembled a man trying to learn how to walk with his shoelaces tied together. He straightened up, shaking his head and cursing. His friend stared at him with a concerned look on his face, apparently unable to speak or act.

I could just make out Sam's face, screwed up in anger and frustration. He looked like a man who could become dangerous, I thought. Better conduct all strategies from a distance. A gun could make him very dangerous indeed.

Sam took a few more steps and fell down, rolling onto his back. He tried to stand but couldn't. His head and arms lifted from the concrete, but his back would not budge. His friend gave him a hand but couldn't lift him from the sidewalk. People began to stop and several of them tried to raise him to his feet, but it was like he weighed a thousand pounds. Sam's friend took off his coat and laid it over a newspaper rack. He was in a frenzy, not knowing whether to call the police, an ambulance or the fire department. Suddenly, Sam stood on his own. He was clearly shaken, frightened. He kept putting both hands on his chest, trying to explain to his friend what it had felt like.

After a few minutes, Sam tried walking again, this time back toward his office building, with his friend hovering at his side like a father teaching his son how to ride a bike. But the going was easy in this direction, and Sam began to relax and to walk more normally. They stopped and talked for a minute and then turned and started back in the other direction again. Sam immediately stumbled and caught himself against the building. His friend rushed over to steady him. Sam was cursing so loud I could hear him from my concealed position across the street. Sam looked at his watch and shook his head. His friend was talking too, probably trying to convince him to call a doctor, or somebody. Sam was so angry he looked like he wanted to strangle his friend. He began walking back toward his office, and this time his friend stayed where he was, just watching Sam to make sure he could make it on his own. Sam had no trouble in this direction and slowly made his way back to the door of his building. He started up the steps, then turned around and looked directly at me. Our eyes met, but I quickly moved my eyes to other people and objects in the area, as if I were just looking around. I walked past my car and turned the corner at the end of the block. I messed around in a dime store for ten minutes, then went back to my car and got away from there.

Everything had gone even better than I'd hoped. The message had been delivered. I'd put Sam through a little training session. And nobody had seen me. I wouldn't even be late picking up my papers. If this didn't scare Sam off, I would just have to think of something more interesting. That was my one concern: had I been severe enough to make my point? Now that it was done, I wasn't sure.

I PULLED UP to the loading dock and jumped out of my car. I wanted to be efficient today. I didn't want to deal with Frank, or anybody else for that matter.

When I got out of the car I felt that difference again, and it was stifling. This place had been strange the day I received the powers, but today there was an eeriness that made me wish I'd called in sick. Everyone, including Phieffer, was deathly silent even though they were working.

But it wasn't so much the silence that made me freeze under the wing of my open door, it was their eyes. When I looked at someone, they looked immediately back at me with a steady gaze, no matter how far away they were or what they were doing. They could feel my eyes on them and turned to look straight at me. They just stared with no expression on their faces that I could read. I wasn't too eager to move away from my car, but I wanted to show them I would not be frightened, would not be intimidated. I kept my eyes averted, found my stack of bundles on the dock, and began to load them into my car, calmly but steadily. I stuffed the last one into the back seat and put my right foot into the car, but before I could slide down into the seat someone grabbed me by the arm and lifted me out the door again.

"Hello Chuck," Phieffer said.

"Keep your goddamn hands off me." I jerked my arm free of his grip.

"Sorry about that." His face remained calm, smiling.

"Yeah, I bet you are."

"All of us just wanted to let you know that we're pulling for you."

Everyone had stopped working. They were all staring at me with that same calm expression. "What are you talking about? What's everybody doing?"

"We all know how hard it is at first."

"Do we have to talk about this now?"

Phieffer moved toward me again, but I stiffened and balled both hands into fists. Phieffer stopped. "We wanted you to know it's okay, Chuck. It'll work itself out."

"Thanks," I said. I looked around at all of them, trying to meet their gaze with that same mysterious confidence. "Tell them I said thanks."

"They know," Phieffer said. His eyes moved away and I turned to follow his line of sight. Frank had appeared on the dock, hands in the pockets of his windbreaker, cigarette dangling from his lips. I just wanted to get the hell away from there.

I climbed into my car and slammed the door.

"Just slow down." Phieffer leaned down to the window. "Just take it easy. Stop pushing."

"Okay," I said, and finding reverse gunned the Bug out of its slot.

"Just remember, Chuck," Phieffer called, "everything you do affects us all."

I turned the car and peeled rubber getting out of the lot.

Those people were getting weirder by the day. I knew I would have to keep coming back at least till the end of the month. Collection day was still two weeks away, and I would need that money. With the money I'd already saved, that would give me enough to live on for three or four months while I was looking for another job, a job that would be more impressive to Sandy. Maybe Mr. B would hire me to help him run the bar. That would be a start, at least.

I PULLED OUT a glass and a bottle of Evan Williams and sat down in my one good chair, adjusting it to the reclining position. I suddenly felt too tired even to eat. Maybe with a few drinks I could block out my dreams and get some real sleep for a change. I poured myself a glass and drank it down, shrugging against the fire that swarmed the pit of my stomach. Within moments I could feel the warmth like a wave sliding onto the shore of my brain. I let my head roll lazily toward the window: the tops of a couple of trees, the tops of buildings like the one I lived in, the thin layering of white clouds far away. I poured another glass and drank it.

MY BODY STIRRED slightly. I was drifting in a world of fragments: faces, corners of rooms, storefronts, the alleys between houses. It felt wonderful not to hold to anything, to let it all drift in and out like the letters in alphabet soup.

Far away, I heard the small sound of metal on metal. I let my body stir, head rolling on the cushion to face the door. I heard that jingle and rattle again, the sound of keys in an old lock. I opened my eyes but the room was dark now and I could see almost nothing in the strands of light that filtered through the window behind me. The door swung open and the silhouette of a girl, or a woman with a girl's figure like my mother's, stood in the doorway. She stepped inside. In the little flecks of light, I could make out the faded jeans, the sweatshirt, the long straight hair. She walked over to me and dropped a small white ball into my lap. Then she sat down opposite me in the beat-up old chair I'd bought in a yard sale. I wished I had something better for her to sit in. She held herself straight, perfectly still, legs together and hands in her lap. I squinted at her but she was still just a silhouette. I felt the light slither out of my eyes and the door swung shut. The lock turned.

I picked up the ball. It was a damp wad of paper that she'd rolled into a perfect sphere. I uncrumpled it, flattened it out on my thigh, then held it up to a spot of light from the window. The letters were smeared and scratched away, but I could tell it was my note. I tossed it on the floor.

"You look like a sleepy king sitting there," she said, "a brutal king, one that can cause the suffering of others with the flick of a wrist."

"I don't expect you to love me right now."

"That's insightful of you."

"Did you tell him about me?"

"Yeah, I told him. He ate it up like a dog with a nice juicy bone. And you know what he said?"

"What?"

"He said maybe we shouldn't see each other for a while. Isn't that funny?"

"Are you drunk, Sandy? You know what the booze does to you."

"So your scheme worked to perfection. You have turned a kind, gentle man into a frightened, scatterbrained idiot. It's the same thing that happened to you, all over again. He even talks about wanting to meet you. Like adding links to a chain."

"Sandy, you're not making any sense . . ."

"Oh, right, and I guess you're all clarity and wisdom."

"If you'd only listen. You never give me a chance to explain."

"Okay, Chuck. I'm all ears. Justify yourself. Help me see the light."

I shook my head. Now that she was here, I didn't know what to say. I didn't know where to begin.

"I love you. Everything I've done was because I have to have you in my life."

"People kill in the name of love, Chuck. Did you know that?"

"I want you to come back to me Sandy."

"I could never come back to this." She looked around. "I can't stand the smell of the place."

"I don't mean here. I can't stand this place either. I've got two more weeks on the route. I just want to collect one more time. I've saved up a little money, enough for the two of us to start over. Sandy, I want the same things you want."

"Do you think I could turn you loose on any child of mine? I could never have a child with you."

"You make me sound like some kind of monster."

"That's what you are Chuck. A very, very small, very ugly monster."

"I don't think you believe that." I stretched up to the lamp beside the chair and flicked it on. My head pounded from the whiskey. I looked at her for a minute. Her shoulders slouched forward now, arms still tucked against her sides, legs squeezed tightly together. Tears streamed down her face and she dabbed at her nose with a Kleenex. But there was no mascara, no make-up.

"You've come back to me haven't you? You're just trying to make it hard for me, to punish me. I don't blame you."

She shook her head. "No. I mean yes, that's what I started out to do. I scrubbed my face. I brushed my hair out the way you like it. I put on these old clothes. But the second I opened that door I knew I couldn't go through with it. I just can't put on those old feelings anymore. They don't fit. At first I thought I had to do it, to save Sam from all of this garbage, and maybe I thought I could help you become human again, like you used to be. But it wouldn't work. It would only make all three of us miserable. This thing has just got to run its course. You've got to do what you feel is right, like all of us. I just don't have it in me to be anybody's savior, or any grown man's mother either."

"I don't want you to be my mother."

"But now that I'm here, I know I could never sleep with you again. I could never let you put your hands on me. The thought of that makes me feel very scared, very sick inside."

"I don't believe that."

"I don't expect you to."

"You're just trying to hurt me, trying to get back at me."

"You're wrong Chuck. I don't want to hurt you. I just want to be perfectly honest with you. No more protecting you, no more being kind, because I know you're not going to be kind to Sam, or to me either. I could see the kindness going out of you before I left."

"The only difference in me is that I've learned some things."

"Well you've sure fooled me. I thought you were a sweet guy, one of the sweetest. That's why I loved you, why I put up with this shithole you live in. All I can see now is a bully, like the bad guys in an old Western, the ones who like to shoot at people's feet to make them dance."

"I'm not like that . . ."

"Then what are you doing with Sam?"

"I'm just trying to bring you back to me."

"What a stupid, mean way to do it."

We sat in silence for a while. Neither of us could look at the other.

"One of your people came to see me this morning," she said.

"What do you mean? Who?"

"A woman. She looked . . . I don't think I've ever seen anyone look out of themselves the way she did, like she was accounting for everything, sewing everything together with her eyes. I knew she was one of you. She reminded me of Frank, had long black hair with a lot of gray in it."

"What did she want?"

"I don't know. But when she saw me it really scared me. I knew I was what she was looking for. She sat down in the chair beside my desk. I tried to believe she just wanted to see my boss. She kept chatting with me about the weather, the news, stuff like that. Finally I told her I couldn't keep talking because I had to get some work done. The next thing I knew, she was gone."

"You should stay away from her."

"Don't worry. I'm going to stay away from all of you."

She stood up and walked over to the door.

"Is there any chance you could just leave us alone?" She turned around to face me.

"I don't know if I can do that. "

Sandy turned toward the door. "Chuck, I can't get the door unlocked."

"I don't want you to leave."

"Are you going to hold me prisoner?"

"Please stay with me tonight. I'm so tired of being alone."

I reached out with the light and encircled her. I wanted it to be nurturing, consoling. I pulled her toward me, one step, then another.

"Are you going to force me?" Her voice was shaking. "Are you a rapist now too?"

"You know I would never hurt you."

"But you *have* hurt me. He was in love with me Chuck. And you want to know something? We haven't even slept together yet. We were still courting like a couple of teenagers who wanted to make love, but weren't quite ready yet. Now he's all messed up in the head. I don't know what's going to happen. If you would just leave us alone."

"I don't want to hear any more of this." The door lock turned behind Sandy. "You can go now."

"The male ego," she said, "is a disease."

She paused as she went out the door, the profile of her face a beautiful silhouette against the light in the hall. For just a moment I thought she was going to come back inside, but then she left, closing the door behind her.

Chapter Eleven

IT WAS ONLY nine-thirty when I got to my car. I couldn't seem to find my keys, then did, head still thick from the whiskey. I had another bottle tucked under my arm. Some kids on the corner were laughing at me, but I glared at them, the light building behind my eyes, and they shut up. I buried them in a cloud of exhaust and headed into the maze of city streets I'd come to know so well. The driving skills I'd developed as a paper carrier made me feel I knew the best route to anywhere in the city, and tonight I wanted to waste no time. I kept having a vision of taking Sam apart with my bare hands, but I knew it wouldn't be like that. I would never lay a hand on Sam. He would never even see my face, if I didn't want him to. He had broken the most important rule, and he had to pay for it, if my word was going to mean anything.

Taking a drink from the bottle, I turned onto Shoreline Drive, a long, winding, suburban two-lane that followed the eastern shore of Lake Gwendolyn. The homes were built on a grand scale fifteen to twenty years ago, huge lots full of old trees, great expanses of lawn, circular drives trimmed with lights revealing a Mercedes or two, maybe a Saab or a BMW, the houses themselves sprawling among the hardwoods like the bodies of sleeping giants, windows full of light and movement. I liked the incongruity of my beat-up 1970 Beetle chugging along this street, 200,000 miles under its belt and still going strong. Through the trees, I glimpsed the shimmering serenity of the lake, boat houses and docks fingering out from the shore. This is what I could give to Sandy, if she wanted it. And she did want it, but not from me. She wanted to be the wife of a doctor or a lawyer, not the wife of a . . . psychic or whatever, no matter how famous or successful. It was my own fault, I knew, for giving her the wrong impression of the powers, of what was happening to me.

At the end of Shoreline, I passed through the stone gates of Manitou Park, a cluster of expensive, two-story condos. I found 211, but turned the corner and parked my car down the street. I strolled toward Sam's condo with my hands in my pockets. The grounds were immaculate, a lilac hedge between each building, neatly trimmed squares of lawn as smooth as putting greens, young aspens carefully arranged, and the street totally free of trash. Through curtained windows I could see the square glow of televisions, could hear the muffled thump and flow of mellow rock, and the driven, dramatic flourishes of Beethoven.

I stopped across the street from 211. The lights were on downstairs and up. I took out the piece of paper and tossed it into the air like a homing pigeon. It drifted across the street and settled on the stoop of 211. The button for the doorbell was lighted. That was easy. But no one came to the door. So I swung the front door open. Also easy.

A minute later Sam appeared in the doorway in his boxer shorts and gave a few puzzled glances up and down the street. He noticed the ball of paper, picked it up and shut the door. But only seconds later he opened it again and caught sight of me. Wait a minute, I thought. Why did I do it this way? I wanted him to see me. We just looked at each other for a minute. Suddenly Sam's body jerked and he staggered through the door onto the stoop. He threw his elbows at the empty air as if someone had grabbed him from behind.

"I couldn't lie to her," he said, just loud enough for me to hear. "She would've figured it out anyway."

I didn't speak, I just kept staring at him. Sam grabbed the metal rail and braced himself.

"But what do you want now? I told her we couldn't see each other anymore."

His body lifted, his arms lengthened and pulled his shoulders down in an exaggerated hunch, his fingers stretching to maintain their grasp on the rail, but they couldn't, and he was thrown straight up in the air to the height of his own second story window where the silhouette of a young woman looked out at him. He spun round and round like a dancer on his pointed toe. A woman on the sidewalk saw him and pressed her hands to her face, gasping as if she were trying to scream but couldn't. Then he fell to the brick walkway, catching himself on his hands and knees. "Jesus God!" he cried and rolled onto his back in the grass. His forehead had hit the bricks and blood streamed down his face. He grabbed both legs and groaned.

I suddenly felt weak and dizzy. The strands of power whirled around my head like the blades of a helicopter.

Sam stood up in a crouch, still holding his knees.

"Chuck!" he screamed, "Please!" But before he could say another word something took hold of him. He flailed his arms, hopped in a frantic hobbled dance around the yard, weeping and cursing as if he were possessed. Suddenly he was in the air again, and the woman fell to the sidewalk and didn't move. Sam never stopped fighting, arms and legs grappling with something he could feel but couldn't touch. Then he fell, disappearing into the thick hedge with a loud crunch and crack of limbs.

Sam's pretty brunette secretary, naked and wild-eyed, bolted from the condo and ran around the yard screaming, "Sam! Sam! Sam!" But she couldn't find him. Neighbors began to appear from everywhere. A young man grabbed the crazed girl, but she kneed him in the groin and kept on screaming Sam's name.

"Fucking bastard," I said with a kind of sick satisfaction. I went down on one knee, struggling to stay conscious. I couldn't let myself pass out. That would mean the end of a lot of things. I pulled myself up on an aspen and staggered down the street to my car.

"Hey buddy, that's a private parking space!" somebody called to me as I crawled into the seat.

When I drove past 211, a sizeable crowd had gathered in the yard. Someone had thrown a robe around the secretary, had calmed her down, but no one seemed to know where Sam was. A couple of people were assisting the woman who had fainted. She was sitting up in the grass, holding her head, talking frantically.

I drove straight home and went to bed with my bottle. I did something then that I've always regretted. I didn't think. I didn't let myself feel anything either. This wasn't a new power, but an old one.

I knew I had to get some rest.

IT WAS A DISTINCTLY feminine voice, calling me from out of a white mist, gently coaxing me to answer. "Charles? Where are you Charles?"

I moved my arms and legs, tried to wake myself.

"Charles, I've come to help you. Don't run away."

I sat up in my bed. I knew I wouldn't be able to sleep any more. It sounded like the spider's voice. I was tired of playing this game, not to mention scared out of my wits. If I could just last two more weeks, I could collect my money and get away from this town, away from Frank and his crowd. Then I could rest up and clear my mind and start over again. With or without Sandy I would have to leave. I would come back for her as soon as I was strong enough.

My alarm clock showed 2 a.m. I rubbed my face with both hands. I still felt sick and exhausted, dizzy from the whiskey.

I got dressed and went out for a walk. The second-shifters getting off work were hitting the few open bars. I thought about sitting down with a cold beer, but I knew it would only make me feel worse. Mainly I just walked, withdrawn, seeing only the sights conjured up in my mind, images of Sandy and Frank and Sam. I saw my mother raising herself up from her bed to ask me where I'd gotten my paper crown. I saw Frank sitting stone-faced in my living room, and the spider up in her corner perfectly still and waiting. I saw Lyuba stalking Sandy just as I'd been stalking Sam. I saw Sam flying through the air over and over, crashing into the hedge. Sometimes I would wake up to the pockmarked sidewalk and the rhythmic placement of one foot in front of the other. I felt almost no physical sensation of walking, but observed the process as if from a distance, like I was walking in my sleep.

Suddenly someone shoved me and pinned me against the wall of a building. It was two boys, no more than fifteen or sixteen, both in black leather jackets and blue jeans. One raised his fist in front of my face and a switchblade snapped open. The boy grinned.

"Give me your wallet," he said.

The other boy looked up and down the street. "Hurry!"

I calmly took note of the knife, the boy's leering face beyond it. Then the boy's face changed, his eyes grew wider, his mouth opened. He took a step back. The arm holding the knife started shaking, and the boy glared at it.

"What the fuck," he said.

"What are you doing?" the other boy said, hopping up and down like an excited fan at a football game.

The boy with the knife backed up against a parked car. He grabbed his right wrist with his left hand and his whole body shook with the effort. His face contorted in a terrible grimace. "I can't stop it any longer," he said glancing at his friend who was still jumping up and down. Then the boy jammed himself in the stomach with the knife and cried out, slumping to the sidewalk. The other boy kneeled beside him. "I'll get help," he said and ran off. His friend was squirming and groaning, blood beginning to pool beneath him.

"Don't fuck with people," I said. Was that really my voice?

The boy opened his eyes and found me through his pain and worry. "Fuck you," he said.

I turned and continued walking up the street. A short time later I heard the sirens, wondered if the boy would make it, and how the two of them would explain what had happened. I smiled to myself. It felt good to know that no one, no matter how strong or quick, could ever hurt me, could even attempt to hurt me without paying a price. But what about the price *I* had to pay? The sleeplessness, the terrible dreams, the sense of being separate from everyone and everything. And Sandy. Wasn't she another part of the price I was paying?

I no longer knew where I was. Places looked different when you were on your feet at night instead of in your car in the daylight. Somehow I had abstracted the world. Everything was distant, untouchable—more idea than object. I kept walking, turning corners at random. My legs grew tired. I had no clue what time it was. The morning's light hadn't yet begun to glow on the horizon.

Then I heard someone call my name. I pulled myself out of the hole of my thoughts and looked around. Not far ahead on the sidewalk, Phieffer stood with his hands in his pockets. I had to laugh. Phieffer wore a white T-shirt and white jeans. With his short, light colored hair and his powerful muscles, he was the spitting image of Mr. Clean. He almost seemed to glow, to be superimposed on a phony backdrop of buildings like in a bad movie.

"Chuck," he said, "Are you alright?"

"Peachy keen. How's the toilet bowl business?"

Phieffer shook his head and laughed. "You sure do have a wacky sense of humor."

"Wacky. Now there's a good word."

"Frank wants to talk to you," Phieffer said, changing his tone.

"Is that so? Kind of an odd time of the night isn't it?"

"Kind of, but it's important."

"Well, I'm sort of busy right now. Places to go, people to see. I'm sure you know how it is."

"Chuck, you can't keep avoiding us forever."

"Why not? It's a free country ain't it? I can avoid anybody I damn well please."

"I hope you're not going to make things any harder on yourself. You really do look beat."

"Should I take that as a threat?"

"Yes," Phieffer said, never taking his hands from his pockets, "in a friendly sort of way. I've got to take you to Frank, one way or the other. I'd like for us to go together as friends, but it's up to you."

"Friends huh? A man who talks tough has to back it up."

"We've got to get you off the streets before you do something else. You have come unglued, my friend."

"And I guess Frank wants to stick me back together."

Phieffer shook his head, exhaling heavily. "You really are a pistol, you know that?" He shook his head again. "No more talk."

"Suits me."

Hands still in his pockets, Phieffer walked toward me. I awakened the power deep inside and made it move, encircling Phieffer, spinning like a whirlwind around him until it flew off in the air above his head. Phieffer strolled up and stopped in front of me. I applied the full force of my energy. I could feel the power whirling around me again like it had at Sam's. I started to feel dizzy and weak.

Phieffer looked concerned. He put his hand on my shoulder. "Ease off," he said. "You're gonna blow a fuse."

The air moved around us like a twister, blowing up trash and debris. The street level windows next to us began to rumble, but I could have no effect on Phieffer.

He laughed. "I've heard of breaking wind, Chuck, but this is ridiculous."

My legs buckled, but Phieffer caught me by the scruff of my jacket and kept me standing. "Just lean on me," he said, putting his arm around me, guiding me down the street.

As we got to Phieffer's truck, a patrol car pulled up beside us. I could hear the muffled squawk of the police radio. The cop rolled his window down.

"What are you boys doing out here this time of the night?"

I tried to speak but my mouth wouldn't open. A feeble groan rumbled in my throat.

"My friend has had a few too many, officer," Phieffer said. "I'm gonna drive him home and put him to bed."

The cop looked at me and nodded. "Looks like an excellent idea. Better be quick about it. We've had some rough characters on the loose tonight."

"Thanks for the warning," Phieffer said, helping me into the seat and shutting the door. "We're on our way."

The cop saluted amiably and drove off.

Phieffer got in and started the car.

"How'd you keep me from talking?" I said, stretching my jaw.

"There's still some things you don't know. It would help matters a lot if you'd start thinking of yourself as a beginner."

Something in my head shifted. Suddenly I became acutely aware of the way I'd been acting. I looked at Phieffer. "I think I might've done some terrible things."

He kept his eyes on the road. "Yeah." He glanced at me with a thin-lipped smile.

"Why am I such a vicious asshole?"

Another glance. "I don't know," he said.

The motion of the car as we drove along and Phieffer's relaxed silence made me unbearably drowsy. I tried to stay awake. I wanted to talk to Phieffer, but the energy required seemed more than I could muster. The harder I tried, the sicker I felt. I let myself slump in the seat and fall asleep.

A WEIGHT SETTLED on the bed beside me, and I opened my eyes to the dark-eyed stare of Lyuba.

"Hello, young man." She patted my chest. "How do you feel?"

"Fine," I said, my voice cracking. "Any reason why I shouldn't?"

"Let's just say you didn't look so good when Phieffer and Frank brought you in this morning. You're going to give yourself an ulcer if you don't take better care of yourself."

I tried to sit up, but the sheet tensed like a muscle over my throat and held me in place. "Hey, what is this?"

"I'm afraid you're my captive for a while." She patted my chest again, letting her hand rest there. "You really leave me no choice, you know. You've left something of a bloody trail over the past couple of days. Quite a little monster you've become."

I tried to throw the sheet aside in a sudden burst of energy, but it tightened around my throat and stretched snug over my body like a giant flap of skin.

"Now Charles, you must not overtax yourself. We have to perform a little operation later on, and you need to be at your best."

"What kind of operation?" I was suddenly unable to catch my breath.

She patted my chest. "Not like surgery. Don't worry, you can handle it. We know what we're doing." For the first time, I noticed her teeth. They were white, perfectly formed, and much longer than most, or was I just imagining things?

"I am *not* a monster," I snarled, "and I'm not some animal that you can just experiment on."

"But that's just exactly what you are." She reached up to stroke the hair from my forehead. "An animal, a monster."

"I'll get you for this." I tried to give her my fiercest stare.

She laughed. "Just listen to yourself. You could learn a lot that way."

"What do you expect?" I groaned, unable to move anything but my head now.

"I spoke to Sandy this morning, not long after you arrived."

"I want you to stay away from her."

"It was *she* who called *me*, Charles, not the other way around. I *have* been going round to see her, though, the past week or so. Quite an impressive young woman in her own way. She was very concerned about you and another good friend of hers by the name of Sam Burnett. I left her my card in case she ever needed to reach me."

"Your card?"

"She was really very upset. I came to this room and watched you sleeping while I talked to her. A very dramatic effect, I thought."

"Yeah, dramatic."

"She said you almost killed Sam, broken bones, that sort of thing. And the young lady that was with him is still under care you know. Claims she saw Sam flying around like Superman. And there are other problems: two people saw you there. If they should ever identify you Charles, well, that would be much too close for comfort for myself and Frank and the others. We'd have to pull back for a while, let the wind blow a little sand over the ruins. I'd rather we didn't have to do that, Charles, if you don't mind."

"I don't give a shit about any of you creeps."

"Now now." She stroked my cheek with the backs of her fingers. "I know that isn't true, but let's not argue the point. We may have very little time together, you and I. I'd rather not waste it."

I glanced around the room. It was large with two sleek chairs and a matching couch. On the bedside table there was a dark blue, smoothly tapered object, possibly a phone. Each wall was a different shade of blue, and blue curtains were pulled tight over the one window. The only light came from a bedside lamp shaped like a forearm and hand, bulb shaded by the palm. My eyes came back to Lyuba's face: the hint of a smile, the glint of amusement in her eyes.

Don't be stupid this time, I told myself.

"I think I could be a lot more relaxed about this," I said, "if I didn't feel like I was being eaten by this bed."

"Oh, but Charles, can I trust you, after the way you've been abusing the power? Such a pitiful waste of time and energy."

I shook my head. "Do you consider keeping me a prisoner like this a wise use of the power?"

"Yes, because you have given us no choice. When that young man on the street confronted you with a knife, you had choices."

"It didn't seem like it at the time."

"You could have given him your money, which was all he wanted."

"Easy for you to say. You don't work for a living."

"A less good but still preferable choice would have been to use your power to ward him off. No need to plant that knife in him."

I took myself back to that moment on the street. It was true, I could've put the knife in a tree across the street. I'd done what I wanted to do.

"And of course your actions against Sam, you obviously had other choices in that situation. We still have to behave like humans whenever possible, you know."

"Okay. You've made your point. I don't know why I did those things, exactly."

"Well, we can't have it, you know."

"I do know. You win. I won't cause any more trouble."

"Do you think perhaps this is coming just a little too late, young man?"

"I hope not. What do you want me to do?"

"Oh, don't worry. We have plans for you."

I didn't like the sound of that. But there was nothing I could do about it. I motioned with my chin toward the sheet that was holding me down. "Please call this thing off now. I can't breathe. You can trust me, I promise."

She nodded and smiled, but made no move to release me.

"I've been wanting to tell you something," I said. I swallowed hard.

"Well go ahead Charles."

"Do you remember the time we met in the restaurant?"

"How could I forget? Such a pleasant conversation with such an intelligent young man."

"Exactly. I . . . I want to apologize. It's like, sometimes I can't see past my own hands."

"You, apologize? If only Frank could be here to see this."

"I just don't want you to think that I'm always such a jerk."

She looked at me for a moment, as if there were so many things she could tell me, but wouldn't. "If we weren't already aware of that, we would have dispensed with you a long time ago."

"I really do hate what I've done. I really do want to change, if I can." I felt the sheet relaxing around my body. I needed to think the right thoughts, say the right things.

She spoke very slowly now. "You don't become hollow just by wanting it. This purging, it's a very dangerous time for some people. Do you understand?"

I took a deep breath, and let it out. "I think I do."

She stood up and extended her hand. "Come on then."

I didn't move. "Where are my clothes?"

"I threw them away."

"But why?"

"Shall we say they were no longer presentable. You were quite sick when you arrived, not to mention filthy."

She extended her hand again. But I didn't move.

"I've already seen you, dear. This shyness is only holding us up. Frank will come by later with fresh clothes."

I took another deep breath, pulled the sheet back and climbed out of bed. My feet came down on smooth carpet. She looked me over and smiled.

"The young. They never seem to realize what a gift their bodies are."

I looked at her: long black hair in a single braid down her back. No make-up. Gray jumpsuit. No shoes. Her hands and feet were brown, slender, alive. She was old, but in her mildly threatening manner, she was also exciting.

"Is that the only way you can respond to any woman, young man?"

I just looked at her. Tried to say something, but couldn't find a word.

She took my hand and led me through several rooms of the huge house, everything sleek, modern, simplified. She had me sit down at a small table in a den that adjoined the kitchen. She brought me sandwiches and tea and watched as I ate.

"How can you afford this place?" I ran my eyes over the expensive, probably custom-made furniture.

"I'm a consultant of sorts. There are people who will pay substantial sums for accurate information."

"What kind of information?"

"All kinds. Finish your sandwich."

"I want to know more about the power, where it came from, who discovered it."

"We keep no recorded history of our kind, beyond a generation or two."

"Why?"

"Because . . . we are not another religion."

"Then what the hell *are* we?"

She shook her head. "No. It would only be another way to misunderstand. Come with me." She stood up, reaching her hand out.

I dropped the sandwich in my plate and took her hand. She led me through sliding glass doors to a patio and pool outside in the warm night air. The sky was clear and full of stars. I could see nothing but woods around the house which was built on a side of the mountain overlooking the city.

"This place is unbelievable," I said.

"Yes, it is. Fortunately, we do not have to believe. Eh?"

She stepped out of her jumpsuit and stood before me naked. I could not help staring at her. "Another one of the benefits of the power," she said. "We need much less food, and our bodies tend to stay young."

I nodded in agreement. She sat down in a chair at poolside and patted the seat of the chair next to her. Carefully, I sat down beside her.

"I understand you used to be quite a good diver." She nodded at the diving board at the far end of the pool.

"My mother was really good, a champion diver."

"Yes, but you could have been good too, with her help. But you see, it's not necessary any more. You have another discipline to build on."

She turned and gazed at the pool, lights under the surface illuminating the bottom, the water so still it magnified three aspen leaves near the drain, thin veins clearly visible. In the middle of the deep end, a small gray moth struggled on the water's surface, fluttering in a desperate circle. Lyuba looked back at me.

"Where do you draw the line?" she asked. "That's what we're all wondering. Frank, Phieffer and the rest of us."

I met her stare and swallowed hard. "I don't know what's happening to me." Tears crawled from the corners of my eyes. I tried to breathe evenly, but couldn't. "You know about my mother, don't you, the way she died?"

"We know that you killed her."

"I thought I was doing the right thing."

"Maybe you were," she said. "That's not for me to say. But what about that young man with the knife? What about Sam Burnett? You see, the power forces your hand. It forces this discipline on you. That's why your mother was such a special person."

"Special in what way?"

"There are those who come to the knowledge without entering the 'third room', without going through the physical mutation. Like your mother. She tried to nurture and encourage that same awareness in you. But you weren't ready. I'm not sure you're ready even now, after all you've been through."

I just stared at the water, at that moth still making its desperate little circles. A coolness had entered the air and I was trembling.

"Why don't you go for a swim?" she said. "The pool's heated. It'll warm you up."

"You've got to be kidding."

"No. Go ahead. I want to see a perfect dive."

I looked at the water and shook my head. "I really don't want to get wet."

She spoke slowly and distinctly, as if these were the last words she would ever say to me. "Charles, this is the time when you have to decide. You can go back inside if you want. I'll get you some clothes and we'll have you back in your apartment in fifteen minutes. After that, you'll never be in contact with us again."

"Or I can dive into the pool."

"Yes."

"Then what?"

"Then we go on with that little procedure I mentioned. And Charles, I want you to know it will not be pleasant."

I believed her, the part about not being pleasant. But going back to my old life didn't feel like an option. Maybe I was crazy, maybe I was dreaming the whole thing. Maybe I was in the presence of someone, some *thing*, that didn't wish me well, that only wanted to control and torture me. But I knew I wanted to finish what I'd started for once, whatever it was. I'd already lost everything that mattered to me anyway. I had nothing left to lose. I stood up and walked in front of her and around the pool, still self-conscious under her gaze. I stepped out on the board, testing its spring. It had been a long time, years, since I'd attempted a dive, but I felt rested all of a sudden, full of energy. If I keep it simple, I thought, if I concentrate, I can execute the perfect dive. I carefully measured out my steps to the end of the board and returned to assume my starting position. I breathed deeply. My mind felt clear and at peace for the first time in a very long time. This is the most beautiful place and the most beautiful night, I thought, looking at the surround of trees huddled together in their own darkness, at the dome of stars overhead as it merged with the valley of stars below. I leaned into the rhythm of those steps I'd learned as a child and could never forget, and the timing was perfect: the spring of the board and the spring of my legs threw me high over the water. I'd forgotten that moment of suspension, that place between rising and falling, between two worlds it seemed, a place of silence and emptiness and light. I felt myself pass through something as I started down, a pocket of warm air maybe, and I entered the water . . . clean, I thought, as solid as I ever did it.

The water was warm, almost hot like a sauna. I wanted to spring off the bottom and erupt victoriously into the night air, but I couldn't find the bottom with my outstretched hands. I opened my eyes and could see nothing but bright lights. I swam farther down and knew I'd passed the eight foot depth, but still there was no sign of the bottom. This isn't possible, I thought, but turned and drifted back toward the surface, lungs beginning to ache. I reached the air, but something was wrong. I couldn't lift my head from the water, and my arms felt huge, heavy, like a wet flannel sheet beating uselessly against the water. I was floating now, unable to dive back down and unable to maneuver myself on the surface which clung to me like syrup. It was difficult to get a breath without inhaling water. My eyes also felt huge and were hard to direct, but I managed to find her standing at the edge of the pool, her body an astonishing tower above me, head sleek and shining, that sad and yet amused look on her face. I wanted to call to her, but she disappeared, nothing but one corner of the house and the sky above me now. A great wave roared over me and

I thought I was gone, but instead felt myself lifted from below and I finally managed a good, deep breath. Her hands were on me, one keeping my head above the surface, the other guiding me smoothly through the water. "It's okay," she said, "you're alright. Just relax." I was too disoriented to relax. It was hard to make sense out of anything I saw, just glimpses and flashes: a dark window of the house, the rising slope of the mountain silhouetted against the night sky, a small gray moth fluttering and flopping on a tile. Then she pulled me against her body, the smooth brush of her breasts, her legs locking me in, the bony hardness of her embrace. I lost all freedom of movement and simply let go of it. She was so close against me I couldn't find her anymore, as if she'd engulfed me, swallowed me whole. "It's okay," she said again, her voice almost a whisper, the dry, cold enamel of her teeth against my face. "You're back in the third room. Don't fight, just let it happen." I felt disembodied, floating in a space she'd created with her own body, and couldn't imagine fighting now, even if I wanted to. Then it all began to fade, like a point of light at the far end of a cave: the small splashing of water, her comforting voice, the thick mist of stars in the clear, night sky.

THE MUSCLES OF my eyes ached as they tried to focus. My arms and legs were heavy, and I wasn't sure I had the strength to move them even if I wanted to. I was afraid I was going to want to move them any second now.

I stared into the white convergence of three lines that I knew to be a corner in Frank's living room. I turned my head to the left as far as I could, and a vast space containing huge, rock-like structures opened up beneath me. In a few seconds I began to distinguish shapes and features and located Frank sitting in the big chair and Lyuba and Phieffer on the couch. They sat up straight and were perfectly still like the monuments of a lost civilization. But then I realized they were moving, very slowly. The modulation of their voices was also slow, a deep, distant rumbling like thunder. They were watching the web and discussing what they saw. I thought that I'd dealt with this web business a long time ago.

What concerned me was a soft, distinct voice coming from nearby.

"Charles," it said. "You came back. I knew you would. Unfinished business always brings you back, doesn't it, Honey?"

I felt the web trembling beneath me, and I held my breath, becoming as still as I could. But I knew that nothing could hide me now, that even the beating of my heart created vibrations and betrayed me. I felt her coming in the way I imagined swimmers sometimes sense the presence of a shark before they see it. She appeared under and behind me so suddenly that I wasn't sure what direction she'd come from, a dark shape many times my size, her legs surrounding me like a great cage.

"Keep still, my darling," she said, "or I will have to bite you."

The way she said things made me want to laugh, and it wasn't easy to fight off the impulse. I kept telling myself to stay calm, that I was in no real danger, that this must be a dream because spiders don't speak, or if they do it's not in English. But my body knew that this was no dream. I was awake.

A lobster-like claw clipped a strand beside my face and let it drop free. Soon I was completely free of the web and in her grasp, the prick of her claws more irritating than painful, though I could tell if I resisted they would tear my flesh. Legs and appendages came from everywhere as she turned me over and over like a pig roasting on a spit. Was she inspecting me? Her abdomen was dark and soft and sparsely covered with hairs the size of pine saplings. Smelling of strange chemicals and blood, the hot wind of her breath poured from the center of her body where there were various openings, some of them pulsing like the flapping of wet sheets. Jaws like a pair of huge thighs hung down from her head and beyond them the ends of two fangs like a pair of hatchets. I couldn't see her eyes.

Almost before I knew it, my legs had been tied together. Looking down the length of my body I saw six finger-like protuberances at the far posterior end of her. Strands of silk oozed from them like soft ice cream out of a machine, only much faster. I was already wrapped up to the thighs, and she was working steadily toward my head. I began to twist and scream as loud as I could.

"Now now," the voice said, "you're only going to hurt yourself, and I'm trying so hard to spare you any suffering. Won't you please cooperate?"

But I felt I was going to die if I didn't do something soon, so I thrashed around trying to free myself, knowing the fall wouldn't kill me, but her claws only caught deeper in my flesh and blood streaked across my body. Thunder rumbled far off, and I thought that Frank must have deserted me completely. Strands of silk pinned my arms to my sides. I was totally helpless now. Maybe I've always been totally helpless, I thought. But no, Lyuba had given me a choice, a real one, I believed, even now.

I let my eyes defocus and watched the world spinning by me, the dark malignant cloud of her body, glimpses of vast space and light all around her, the web stretching out and billowing gently, the three planes of the ceiling and walls coming together into a dusty point. I became dizzy and closed my eyes. A part of me was giving up and I tried to resist it, tried to motivate myself, but I knew that my silk straight jacket made any effort futile. The strands closed snugly around my neck, then snapped around my forehead. I stopped spinning and a strange vision appeared before me. The spider held me out in front of her like a baby wrapped in a blanket with only the face visible. Her eyes fixed on me, eight huge, black, shiny bubbles symmetrically arranged into the aspect of a face with the great jaws dangling beneath like walrus tusks.

"I want you to see what it feels like," the voice said, coming more like thoughts than the real articulation of speech.

Then I was under her again, spinning, the strands pulling tight around my face. I was sealed in completely. I could wiggle my toes and fingers slightly, I could move my lips and my nose a little, and my eyelids would open, the lashes sticking to silk. But I could see nothing but darkness. I was, in effect, buried alive. Finally the spinning stopped, and I could feel myself dangling from the web. She was gone.

Already, the warmth of my own trapped body was suffocating. My only concern now was breathing. My lungs filled and emptied, but there was so little oxygen to absorb . . . a heaviness in my lungs, a tightening, a dull ache that was becoming sharper. I was panting, but it did no good. I remembered this pain from the summertime when I was a kid. I and my friends would have contests to see who could stay under water the longest. I usually won. My ego had always been larger than the pain. But this time, as I felt the seconds piling up, I knew there was no shining surface to push to and erupt from in a victorious explosion of water, no lake at all, no friends, no silent surround of trees, no continent of air to lounge in while my mother made her beautiful shapes in the sky.

Sweat stung my eyes. I began to cough and gasp, bringing up the sandwich I'd eaten earlier, the fluids on my stomach which now crept along my neck and chest. I was going, and that was all there was to it. I knew I was going, and I started to give in. Just watch the pain, I thought, just watch the body convulsing, just listen to it turning itself inside out, the heart tightening and winding up, a shaking fist. Just listen to that high pitched tone in your ears getting louder. Just look it in the eye and watch it coming in because it's coming for real this time and it's coming fast and there's nothing you can do to stop it. So put some distance between yourself and the pain, the body, and see what you can see. Just take these last few seconds for yourself and know what you can know.

But as it closed on me, this voice faded. I could only be this body, the incredible tension that filled it. I heard a snapping sound, a pop, a crack in both ears, as something broke loose in my body, like a leather strap breaking under pressure. Had my chest caved in? Had my heart burst? A terrible cold like a brick of ice inside me. And the cold spread over my chest, shoulders and belly, and crept into my loins. I was drenched in blood.

But then the voice, my own voice, calmly coaching me, became stronger. And I began to find separation, the edge of that space I was looking for, that I somehow knew existed, and as my voice grew stronger, that distance between myself and my body grew wider, and the body finally relaxed and became still, the chest falling, expelling that last lung full of blood and carbon dioxide. Then I separated from breathing altogether. Breath was the past I was moving away from. And the voice, unneeded now, disappeared. For a while there were silent, colorful explosions of light. But those fell away into the distance. Then there was nothing, no sensing of anything, only this suspension in a slow river of silence and darkness.

THEN THERE WAS seeing. There was a thin streak of light and it collided with another streak of light and the explosion made more flying off in all directions. They collided with other streaks of light and the explosions made more. There was a complex network of reactions, and the space I was in, whatever it was, began to fill with this light until there was only light and nothing else. The light passed through me, whatever I was, and filled me completely. I was both inside the light and outside of it. I both saw it and was it. It was as bright as the unobscured sun, but soft and warm. There was no fear or loneliness here, only a peaceful feeling that was wide and deep and thick. I liked it here. No more craving and effort and thought. No more touch and attachment. I could live here forever if it were allowed. I felt that I had come home, and there was only this fullness, this fullness of light.

Chapter Twelve

Clothes and magazines littered the floor. A couple of outdated calendars and an old science fiction poster hung on the walls. Gleaming in her bright cartoon colors, a voluptuous, scantily clad woman struggled in the grasp of an alien beast retreating over barren, rocky landscape toward a distant space ship, the rays of his handgun slashing into the darkness that held his enemy.

I had awakened in my own bed. This was not where I wanted to be.

Why didn't they just let me stay dead? I thought.

I closed my eyes. I felt empty inside, alone. But there was another feeling too, a field underneath everything that I'd never noticed before. I would have to explore that. I had awakened once before in this bed with a feeling that everything had changed, that everything was new. Maybe everything is always new and never new all at the same time.

I looked at the clock on my bedside table. Ten o'clock.

Yeah, but what day is it? I thought. I feel like I've been asleep for a week.

I sat up on the side of my bed and my head throbbed. All my muscles and joints were sore, like I'd been dropped repeatedly from a second story window. I was hungry, starving in fact.

I got dressed and walked feebly to the Sha Na Na. I noticed a gray Mercedes parked on the street, windows rolled down, an unusual gesture of trust for this part of town. Everyone on the street drew into themselves, studying their own stream of thoughts and memories, passing each other without the slightest acknowledgement, or if their eyes met accidentally, the quick look away. Almost like machines, I thought, or ghosts functioning in totally different planes, that same old movement of separation and isolation, only it seemed worse now—the opposite extreme of being at the loading dock of *The Sun.* Was there any sort of normal human behavior between these two extremes? The man sitting next to me at the counter had a week-old stubble of beard and smelled of sweat and whiskey. His filthy, strong-looking hands nonchalantly toyed with a hawk's feather on the bar. His pulled-back, greasy hair made him look something like a hawk himself. When his eyes met mine briefly, I nodded and said, "Good Morning." The man gave a low, dismissing chuckle and turned away.

The food revived me, and when I returned to my apartment I was restless. I looked around and realized I couldn't live another day in those rooms the way they were. I opened up a new box of trash bags and began to clean the apartment, picking up piles of old magazines, fast food trash, plastic plates from TV dinners, old clothes too worn or damaged to be used again. I broke down all the cardboard boxes I'd been using as furniture and stacked them in a corner. The old calendars and sci-fi posters also had to go. I dusted the few surfaces that were left and swept the floors three times, trying to remove every speck of dust. I got down on my knees and scrubbed the stubborn places where I'd spilt things. The kitchen was the hardest part, the sink and counters sporting a layer of scum with rock-hard little mountain ranges. I actually enjoyed chiseling away at them. I scrubbed and scraped and wiped and polished and threw away or carefully stored until everything I owned had been touched and accounted for and put into its proper place.

I had no urge to use the powers, though I sensed their potential more strongly than ever before, as if they were swelling inside of me, producing a slightly uncomfortable tightness throughout my body.

When I finished, I fell into my one good chair and relaxed. Against the wall there was a row of giant plastic garbage bags stuffed full and tied off at the top. The old disfigured chairs were stacked to the ceiling. The rooms seemed almost empty now and gave the appearance of someone moving out.

"Well, you *are* moving out," I said aloud.

I looked at the peeling walls and the water-damaged ceiling. In spite of everything, I was going to miss this place. A lot had happened here. I'd been very happy when Sandy was here with me. And there was the day I moved the stone and realized I had the power.

It was one o'clock, time to pick up my papers. I'd apparently missed three days, according to what I'd overheard at the restaurant, and felt eager to get back to the route, especially now that I'd be doing it only a few more times. And only one more collection.

I PULLED INTO the dock and sat in my car for a moment, not wanting to enter again the strange atmosphere of *The Sun*. Everyone was working, removing bundles from chutes and loading them into vehicles. But the silence of their acknowledged unity was thick in the air. I climbed out of my car, and the thread connecting them passed through me as if I were the eye of a needle. I felt it in my stomach and a wave of nausea rolled over me. I was a part of them now, there was no escaping that. I closed my eyes and leaned against my car.

A hand grasped my shoulder. "Chuck, are you alright?"

I turned and looked into the clear, shining eyes of Phieffer. "Not really," I said, "I'm feeling pretty sick."

"Yeah, you do look a little green around the gills. It affects some of us like that for a while, but you'll get over it in a few days."

"I hope you're right, because a few days is all I have. I'm leaving at the end of the month."

Phieffer's eyes glinted in the mid-day sun. His grip tightened on my shoulder. "You're not really going through with that, are you?"

"Yep. Ten more days and I'll be on the road again."

"You can't leave. This is your home now."

I looked around the dock, catching a glimpse of Jeff and John Wallace constructing their monumental load. Mrs. Posselt lifted and tossed her bundles with the strength and energy of a person half her age. My eyes stopped at the door to Frank's office, where the man himself appeared and leaned against the doorjamb, cigarette dangling from his lips. His eyes caught and linked with mine, and I felt the energy flowing between us with a low, almost electric hum.

"Yeah," I said, turning back to Phieffer, "but I never was much of a homebody. Besides, I ought to hate the whole bunch of you after what you did to me."

"You ought to, but you don't."

Phieffer stood aside, and everyone at the dock stopped what he or she was doing and looked directly at me. I didn't know what to do. An unprecedented stare-fest. What were they trying to say to me? This went on long enough that I thought maybe we were on the verge of participating in the first incidence of multiple spontaneous combustion in recorded history. But before the flames came, Phieffer went back to his truck, and the others went back to work. Whenever I was at the loading dock now, whenever I was with any one of these people—Phieffer, Frank, Lyuba—it was as if I'd entered an alternative dimension in time and space, a dimension that somehow intersected with the ordinary one I'd lived in for most of my life. The impossible, as I knew it to be, became possible. Why was I trying to explain all of this? I'd read way too much science fiction, and those were the only terms I had to help me. The fact was, I no longer knew with certainty what was real and what was unreal.

I loaded my car as quickly as possible without seeming to rush. I knew I wanted to belong to someone, to something, but I also knew that this wasn't it. All I could think about was getting away, as far away as I could.

A WEEK BEFORE the end, Frank sent a young man named Pat to ride the route with me. He had a blue tattoo of a naked woman on his right forearm. He wore a plain white T-shirt no matter the occasion. He smoked Camels constantly and wasn't much interested in helping me roll the papers or in learning the route for that matter. He mostly just stared out the window with narrowed eyes and occasionally muttered something abusive at the traffic or a pedestrian.

Jesus, I thought, where did Frank dig this one up? I wondered if Frank had plans to bring him into the family. He sure would be a tough case to handle. A deep preoccupation was written all over the young man's angular features. I laughed, imagining the look on this fellow's face the first time Frank played one of his "tricks" on him.

I asked to have the route to myself for a couple of days. I was tired of breathing Pat's smoke and having to deal with his sullen unwillingness to help. Besides, I wanted to be alone with the route, which had probably been my best friend for the past few years, my mindless escape into routine. I loved my intricate knowledge of these streets, the back alleys, the shortcuts, the alternative routes when traffic was bad. And I knew something of the people too, though mainly that small part of themselves they chose to show to the likes of paper boys. But occasionally I got a glimpse of more as I stood on their porches or in their front rooms waiting for them to get my money. I saw the objects they chose to have around them. I witnessed brief interchanges between husband and wife, between parent and child, and I came to know them to a degree.

Finally, it was the first of the month and the last time I would have to collect. And I would have to ride out with Pat one more time to make sure he had the route under control. I helped him load the bundles into his battered Camaro and got out of there as soon as I could, wanting no scenes with Frank or Phieffer. Frank remained his usual background presence in the doorway of his office, and Phieffer merely shook my hand and slapped me on the shoulder. They seemed as willing to let me go now as I was to leave. Besides, I'd realized a long time ago that my connection with them wasn't personal in the usual sense. I wasn't sure there was a word to describe that relationship. I decided I'd write Frank from time to time to let him know how things were going. And who knows, I might even come back to Colorado Springs someday.

I was very impatient with Pat on the route that day. I couldn't stand his dawdling style behind the wheel, and the way he would stop and roll a paper for each house when he got there. This'll take all day, I thought. Pat made no objections when I just took control. I had him pull over and I got behind the wheel myself. Then we rolled all the papers at once. My hands were quick and strong, like a pair of highly trained little animals, and my stack of rolled papers grew fast. Pat grunted and groaned and went through all kinds of contortions to get a paper rolled, then he rested and smoked a cigarette. I wondered how the hell he was ever going to do this thing by himself.

I decided I'd give him a small demonstration of the power, just to see if I could wake him up a little. I started making unusually accurate throws, back-handed with my left hand from the driver's window, or over the top of the Camaro. At first Pat just mumbled "nice throw," but then he suddenly sat up straight in his seat. I tossed one over the top and it landed in the middle of a yard, scrambled up porch steps and came to a halt standing on its end just outside the front door.

"Hotdamn!" Pat said, a long ash from his cigarette falling into his lap. "How did you do that?"

"It's a special service I provide, for my better tipping customers."

"Oh," Pat said. But then he shook his head. "No. I mean how did you make that paper do that?"

"It's all in the follow through." I demonstrated my throwing motion, and Pat mimicked me. "You have to get the right spin on it."

"Spin," Pat said laughing. "There ain't no spin that would do that."

"It just takes practice."

Pat was much more alert, and much better company, for the rest of the route. He even made a few good throws himself.

When we finished the route Pat dropped me off at my car. Fortunately it was late spring and the days were getting long. There was still plenty of daylight left. I had already gone out that morning and collected from most of the businesses and office buildings. Now I looped back to the suburban sections that were the dependable core of my route. When I let them know this was my last day, many tipped me especially well and told me I'd been the best paper boy they'd ever had. It was a small matter, but still I was proud. It was the one job I'd ever done really well. I moved on to the three mobile home courts and chalked up about eighty percent, which was good for the first time through. Even Mrs. Higgins paid up with a modest tip. She patted my hand and wished me luck. Then I started picking my way through the rent-by-the-day-week-or-month motels and the massage parlors and porn shops that surrounded them, and my percentages dropped way off, but that was to be expected. When I finished, I started back at the beginning and tried to catch the ones I'd missed the first time. A light rain started to fall, but the air was still warm and I had a good jacket with a hood to keep me dry. At least it wasn't winter, when I'd be dealing with snow and tire chains.

It was well after dark when I finished. The light rain had turned into thunder showers that passed through quickly, leaving the streets wet and the air clear and cool, the streetlights and the lights from signs and windows sparkling. As I stepped out of the hot, spicy air of the oriental massage parlor that was my last collection, a gray Mercedes with tinted glass rolled slowly in front of me. Water beaded up on the hood and roof, a ghostly face barely visible in the driver's window. I noticed a number of expensive cars parked along this street, my own beat-up VW sandwiched between a Cadillac and a large, late model Oldsmobile.

I was exhausted, but still I decided I needed to talk to Frank before getting some sleep. I'd be leaving tomorrow, and I knew I wouldn't feel right about it if I didn't see him one more time. I stopped off for a quick bite to eat, and then I headed for Frank's house.

I PULLED UP to the curb and killed the engine. I figured I was look-ing at this house for the last time, this neat white clapboard, always dark and quiet. Frank's blue Ford was in the carport. I walked across the fresh-cut lawn, around the side of the house, through the metal gate and into the back yard where Frank was waiting, sitting next to that same table, the cooler, another chair. He was looking up at the night sky, clear now, speckled with stars.

Two bottles of beer were on the table, flecks of ice still sliding down the glass.

"Expecting somebody?" I said.

"He just arrived," Frank said, still staring at the sky.

I sat down and took a drink. "Damn, that's good."

Frank turned toward me, and his pupils were so enlarged that I'm sure he couldn't see me.

"Are you okay?" I said.

"Never better."

I looked up at the stars and could feel that ancient light gathering in the air around me. Does light gather? No. But that's what it felt like. Then I looked back at Frank. His eyes were almost normal again.

"You have some questions," Frank said, taking a crumpled pack from his breast pocket, tapping a cigarette on the metal arm of his chair.

As always, he was ahead of me. How long had I known this man? "I can't tell what's real anymore," I said.

"That's easy," he said. "Nothing's real. Same as saying everything's real. Which means, you have to stay very alert."

I stared at him. I wanted to laugh. "So that's it?"

"You were expecting more? Be hollow. Stay alert. It's the only way I know."

I took a long pull on my beer and emptied the bottle. Then I wrestled another cold one from the cooler.

"How many of these things do you drink every night?" I asked.

"Oh, maybe three or four."

"Does that help you with the being alert part?"

Frank laughed. "Yeah, I guess it does."

"Just one more question," I said. "I feel like something's snapped inside. I mean, I feel like I should hate you and your mother for what you did to me the other night. But I don't. It's almost like it was somebody else."

"You're just beginning to see through things a little, that's all."

I shook my head. "Whatever you say."

We drank in silence for a few minutes, then Frank looked at me. "So where are you going?"

"I thought I'd go home and see my family. After that, I don't know."

"I was kinda hoping you'd stay around here."

"I never was much of a joiner, Frank."

"This new kid, Pat, he was gonna be your project, you know."

I shook my head. "I don't know about that guy. I think you've got a tough one on your hands."

"I've seen worse."

"Come on Frank. I ran that route like a pro. Did you ever get any complaints on me?"

"A couple."

"Only because you kept me away and *you* had to deliver."

Frank screwed up his face and laughed. "Anyway, I wasn't talking about the fucking route."

"Oh," I said. "That."

"Yeah. That."

I considered it for a moment. "It's tempting, but I don't think I could handle Pat."

"Maybe not." Frank grimaced through a cloud of his own smoke. "You may be right."

He turned and gazed at the stars again. He dropped his cigarette in a half-filled ashtray in the grass beside his chair. He leaned back and became very still. I relaxed and looked at the stars myself, but I could hardly keep my head up or my eyes open. After a while I reached over and tapped Frank on the shoulder, but he didn't move. I shook his arm, but the body was limp. I pressed my ear to his chest. I couldn't hear a pulse, but he was breathing, slow and steady. His eyes were partially open, dilated again and black as the night. It was as if his body were no more than a husk or a shell. How do you respond to something like that? How are you supposed to feel about it? Was the man Frank Posner sitting in that chair? Had some significant part of him vacated the premises? Did I ever want to be this vulnerable, this hollow? Frank Posner had left the building, and so did I.

I walked back to my car, the damp grass shining in the starlight. In a large puddle, I saw a small gray moth struggling on the surface.

I scooped it out and laid it in the grass, wings still pulsing frantically. Would it have lived or died just the same no matter what I did? I didn't know, but I was glad I'd done something. I could feel this deep and permanent transformation inside my body. Every moment felt alert in and of itself, no matter what I chose to do. Every moment had this weight of significance.

As I opened my car door, I noticed the gray Mercedes parked on the street half-way down the block behind me. This was not a Mercedes neighborhood. I stared at the dark windshield for a while, but there was no movement. I couldn't imagine any reason for someone to follow me. I got in my VW and started up. When I rounded the corner at the end of the block, the headlights of the Mercedes blazed on.

I SPENT THE next day clearing up details. I sold my one good lounge chair to a neighbor for twenty bucks. Then I broke up my three-legged chairs and tables, loading them into my landlord's pickup to be used for firewood. I packed my car with the few belongings I had left, finding that smooth round stone that Frank had given me in the pocket of an old pair of jeans. Holding its cool weight in the palm of my hand, I remembered the day that it had flown around my rooms like a remote controlled hornet.

Using a neighbor's phone, I had the electricity taken out of my name, then drove into town to close out my savings and checking accounts and clear up a few small debts. I went to the omelet restaurant for lunch, half hoping I'd see Sandy there. That evening, with all of my business finally taken care of, I splurged on dinner at a seafood restaurant on the edge of town. Taking my time, I drank a couple of extra cups of coffee after the meal, hoping the caffeine would help me stay awake. I would drive as long as I could, then pull off in a parking lot somewhere and sleep until morning. Three long days on the road were staring me in the face.

When I climbed in behind the wheel of my car, I realized that my hands were shaking and my heart was pounding. Maybe it was the caffeine. Maybe it was the fact that Sandy's apartment was only two miles out of my way.

I stopped at a pay phone and dialed her number. It rang several times before she answered.

"Hello."

"Sandy, this is Chuck."

"Oh. What do you want?"

"Listen, I'm on my way out of town. I just wanted to stop by and say good-by, if it's okay."

She covered the phone with one hand. I could hear two voices, indistinct.

"I ought to have my head examined," she said, "but okay. I can introduce you to someone."

"Someone?"

"Mike," she said. "You'll like him."

Before I could tell her I'd changed my mind, she'd hung up.

She'd rented a house in one of those new neighborhoods on the outskirts of town. Housing for low-income families. She always did like being outdoors, hiking, views of the mountains and the plains. Children running around. It was all here. I parked my car across the street. Two cars in her drive-way. A small brick house with a picture window. I could see the two of them sitting at the dining room table. I just watched them for a while. Cups of coffee. Something on the table between them: a book or an atlas—they kept tapping it with a forefinger, turning a page. They were waiting on me. What would be the point of going in? What could I possibly say to her with someone else there? After a while she looked at her watch, then up and out the window toward me. She got up, stretched, pulled her hair back from her face, and walked through her living room toward the window. As she crossed the room, the overhead light caused her features to flare into view for a moment—how does a face—how do eyes—come to mean so much? Then she passed under the light and her body darkened. She leaned against the window, a silhouette now. I don't know for sure if she could see me, but I think she could, because she just kept on staring out the window, with Mike at the table behind her engrossed in his reading. She cupped her hands around her eyes and pressed against the glass. I decided on a final and perhaps dramatic gesture. A generous one, I hope. I started my Beetle and drove away.

I STOPPED AT the first gas station I came to, gassed up, found a row of payphones at the edge of the lot. I called my home in South Carolina. My father could not believe at first it was me he was talking to. He thought I was dead, or worse. He cried. I cried, tried to tell him how sorry I was. It didn't matter, he said, it didn't matter, just come home. I talked to one of my brothers. Come home. "And by the way," my father said to make sure I wouldn't be surprised when I arrived, "I've married again. A wonderful woman," he said. He was certain I would love her. I was certain, too.

MY STEPMOTHER WAS a generous and kind woman, and I did love her. I had run away from home at the age of fifteen because I had killed my own mother. I returned home at the age of twenty-two to a new mother. I was still a young man, but with no prospects. I worked for my father at the car lot, cleaning up, changing tires, running errands. Sometimes, when one of the salesmen called in sick, I got to sell a little. And I studied. Got my GED within a couple of years. But I knew I didn't want to sell cars the rest of my life, and my father understood.

A carpenter in my father's church took me on as an apprentice. For a long time I was a gofer, a wielder of shovel and pick, a hod carrier, the one who did the clean-up work after others on the crew had gone home for the day. But people get sick or die or simply move on, and I got my chance to drive nails, to climb up to the roof and put down shingles, to pour concrete in what would be the basement floor, to frame the house, to lay brick, put up drywall. And after a few years I became an indispensable member of the crew. I cannot tell you how good that felt, to become a part of something, a kind of family of people working toward the same goal. And after a few more years I had my own crew, became a builder respected in the community for my good work, and I have felt like a king of sorts for years. Not a great king with the power of life and death, whose commands lie heavily on the lives of thousands, but a king in the sense of lucky in the most ordinary of ways. Lucky in the ways that I thought were not possible for me—to live a productive life among friends and family.

Those slim hands of mine that my mother said were the hands of an artist have grown thick and callused with my work. But I do sometimes feel like an artist. I love driving around the county and seeing those houses that I built with these hands. I love starting a new house, the challenges of fitting it to the land, of solving the thousand problems that arise. The discipline. I love watching that house rise up and breathe, as close to a living thing as anything a man can build. And there is nothing better than seeing a family moving in to a house that I've built. I've taken to drawing my own house plans, and people seem to like them, which makes the houses feel more like my own than ever before.

My father says I should get out of building the houses myself, hire crew bosses, maybe have three crews, and build a lot more houses, maybe have an office in town with a secretary. I know I could do this and maybe become a rich man, but I'm afraid that would only bring me back to my old pettiness and callousness, make me the wrong kind of king. Besides, I'm afraid to stop doing what I love most to do, which is being out there with my men building that house with our own hands. And I love bringing some young man or woman onto the crew and seeing them learn and become good at something that makes a difference. It took me so long to find what I love to do, I'm not going to take any chances. Besides, I have everything I want. My wife and I live in a mobile home on five acres of land out in the country. For now, it seems like enough. And behind that mobile home she and I are building our own house with our own hands. I hope it will take us a long time.

FIVE YEARS AFTER leaving, I went back to Colorado Springs. I don't know what I expected, but whatever it was, I didn't get it. *The Sun* was on its last legs as a newspaper, circulation down to half what it had been when I was there. At first no one seemed to remember Frank Posner, but then I ran into Mr. Holloway himself, and of course he remembered Frank. Disappeared about five years ago. Ran out on his contract and the paper was going to sue him but they never could find him. There were rumors he'd gone to Minnesota. Posner, as Holloway referred to him, most definitely did not own the paper, a ludicrous idea, and no one in Posner's family, if he even had a family, had anything to do with the paper. Phieffer, the Wallaces, Mrs. Posselt, all of them had left the paper around the same time. Had left Colorado Springs too, if area phonebooks were any indication. I knew I could find them, or at least some of them, but it would take time. Did they want me to find them? Frank's house was occupied by a couple with three small children.

And Lyuba—I had never known where her house was. I stayed in town for a week, and each day I drove around in the wealthy neighborhoods that had the kind of elevation that I remembered. I did find a house that could have been hers—it had the pool, the same view, the right kind of architecture—but the furniture, the carpets, and the people were not right. Nice people, though, believing the story I told about growing up in that house.

I even went back to the Mayfair Restaurant for lunch. Sure enough, Maggie was working The Green Room. I waited until I could get a table in her section. She whizzed by, slapped a menu on my table, saying "I'll be with you in a minute." She looked the same as the last time I'd seen her when Sandy and I had shared our last meal together. Maybe her face showed a few more lines. Maybe there was the slightest touch of gray in her hair. But she looked vigorous as she dropped off some more menus, delivered drinks, took an order, her stride purposeful, almost athletic. Finally she returned to my table, took out her pad and looked at me for the first time. She kept on looking at me and smiled.

"I remember you."

"I'm glad to hear that."

"You used to be a regular. How long's it been?"

"Five years, more or less."

"Damn, where'd you get to?"

"South Carolina."

"I've always wanted to go to South Carolina. Hell, I've always wanted to go anywhere. What'll you have?"

I ordered. And that was the most words that passed between us. It was the middle of the lunch hour and she was very busy. It was just good to see that she was still going strong, no more worse for wear than the rest of us.

All of this was little more than delay tactics. Finally, my last day in town, exhausting every contact I had, I found Sandy—married, of course—and called her. On the phone she said, "Yes, of course I remember you." And it must've been true because she invited me to stop by. "You're not gonna run out on me again this time, are you?"

I didn't run out, but maybe I should've. This time she lived on Shoreline Drive in a big ranch style house. Paved horseshoe drive-way down to the front door. Landscaping. She welcomed me with a hug. Her husband Mike was a doctor, an orthopedic surgeon, she said, and he was at the hospital. Two kids: two-year-old son, four-year-old daughter. For a moment they were wary of the stranger and clung to her as we retired to the living room and comfortable chairs. Then they began to play with some toys on the floor, and Sandy and I talked for maybe half an hour. I can't remember much of what we said, mostly small talk. Her memory of Frank and Lyuba was vague; she called them my "mysterious friends." She talked about my old apartment, about us; these were good memories for her, a fact for which I'm very grateful. My feelings, as I sat there, talking in such a relaxed way, with her children laughing and rolling on the floor, were strong, and many. But what were they? Desire, regret maybe, gratitude, and unnameable loss. All rolled up together, they felt like the pain of love. She was working two days a week in a research lab, taking some classes part time to finish her degree. Science was still her first love. Maybe she would be a doctor too, eventually. But she had wanted more than anything to be a great mother. She had created the circumstances in which she could be exactly that.

As I left her house, she stood in the doorway and cocked an eyebrow. "Where's your old Beetle?"

"Gone the way of all things," I said, and climbed into my late model, mid-size Honda.

Compulsively clicking the release button on my handbrake, I drove my faithful old VW Beetle through the familiar outskirts of Colorado Springs toward the interstate that would pull me due east to South Carolina and my home town of Rock Hill. It had been so long since I'd been home I didn't know what to hope for. I rolled both front windows down, and the cool air swirled around me. I would've turned the radio on too, if it worked, anything to help keep me awake. I'd grown accustomed to the mild summers of Colorado Springs and wasn't sure I was going to like the 95 degree temperatures and 90 percent humidity of a South Carolina June.

It almost felt like I was running away. Running away the first time had not helped me escape my mother. I would always hate her and love her and miss her just as I was already missing Sandy. I was addicted to people and didn't want to fight it anymore. Even Frank needed other people, in spite of his emptiness, in spite of the third room and the other lives he lived there. Wasn't that why he'd created his own special family? Never mind his mother, Lyuba, who no longer seemed human to me.

For old times' sake I detoured along one of *The Sun*'s weekend truck routes I used to drive on occasion as a substitute. One by one I passed the empty corners where I'd dropped bundles, some kid with a bike emerging from the shadows to pick up his load for the morning route. Out here the lots were larger, the houses farther apart, the roads sometimes unpaved. German Shepherds lunged against chain link fences surrounding trailers or small houses that had sprouted on the treeless prairie like mushrooms. I pulled off the blacktop and followed a dirt road through the future site of a housing development. The road gained altitude quickly and soon became little more than a path that ran along a barren ridge. I turned off my lights and geared down, the Beetle scrambling over the rough ground like its namesake. When I reached the highest point, I parked at the edge of the worn circle where kids with dirt bikes had turned around and headed back down the ridge.

I climbed up on the front of my car, using the hood and windshield as a lounge chair, and gazed into the thick mist of the Milky Way. It wasn't sleep I craved, or food, or sex or anything else I could name. For a moment I felt myself being wrapped by the spider again, the claustrophobic encircling of the power. But this time I didn't resist it. This time the thread was not of silk, but of light. I let it drive my breath away like so many stray cattle on the plain. My heart drifted down into a cool, comfortable hole and slept like a child. But my eyes didn't sleep. The light poured into me and out of me in a stream that connected to everything around me, the distant lights of homes, the sage trembling in the wind, pronghorn just out of sight on the ridge's slope, and someone who was approaching me, slowly. The light filled me and seemed to swell beyond all boundaries, consuming everything, until the light was all there was. Maybe this was where Frank had been leading me, maybe this was what I was supposed to find. For the first time in my life, I wasn't afraid. It wasn't that I felt invulnerable. I knew that I could die, like anybody else. I could have a wreck, or someone could catch me off guard and shoot me. And I would die. The light would be squeezed out of me just like anyone else. But now at least I knew that the light existed and that it was indestructible. I knew that no matter what happened, some part of me would be connected to the world.

I BECAME AWARE of some disturbance in my body, and I slowly withdrew myself from the light. Something stabbed my arm, then shook it.

"What's the matter with you?" a man's voice said. "Are you dead, or just dying?"

I rolled my head and saw the man standing next to the Beetle, a gray Mercedes with tinted glass parked behind him. The man's mouth dropped open and his eyes grew large.

"What happened to your eyes?" he said. "Chuck, are you okay?"

The man was holding a gun. I sat up. Light fell over him and curved around him. His face was swollen and bruised, his forehead bandaged. It was the omelet-man, Samuel T. Burnett, attorney at law, wearing jeans and tennis shoes and a white dress shirt with big circles of sweat under the arms.

"No wonder Sandy was so scared," Sam said. "You've got the wildest damn set of eyeballs I've ever seen."

"I thought you'd still be in the hospital," I said.

"I bet you did. Nah. A few busted ribs, chipped bone in the arm, knees swollen up. Hell, I've been worse hurt after a football game."

"You played football?" I was stalling for time, trying to re-orient myself. The light in Sam looked as if it might explode any second.

"Damn right. Linebacker at Colorado State."

"What's with the gun?" It kept bursting into flame under the starlight.

"Figured I might need an equalizer before this night was over." Sam grinned, but without any sign of humor in his pale eyes.

"Okay, but that gun won't cut it."

"I guess we're gonna find out about that. Stand up."

I stood up.

"Empty your pockets."

"You mean you followed me all the way out here just to steal my money?"

"Just shut up and do it."

I took a step toward Sam, and he took a step back.

"Stop right there." But I kept on walking.

"I warned you," Sam said and pulled the trigger. But the gun didn't fire. Sam held it sideways and looked at it. The hammer was pulled back and wouldn't release, no matter how hard he squeezed the trigger. He pointed it at me again.

I stopped a foot away from Sam, the gun barrel pressed against my stomach. I smiled again and leaned against the end of the gun so that Sam had to hold me up.

"You can't hurt me with that gun," I said.

Sam backed against his car. He reached down with his free hand to the handle, never taking his eyes off me, but the door wouldn't open. "Goddamnit!" he screamed, jerking on the door. Then suddenly his grin turned into a grimace of pain, and the gun fell out of his hand onto the ground. "Jesus," he said, grabbing his hand. He looked at the gun, then back at me.

"You shouldn't take the Lord's name in vain like that," I said, laughing.

"Are you gonna start preaching at me now?" Sam held his hand as if it had been shot.

I picked the gun up. "No. I'd rather just shoot you." I cracked the gun open, emptied the bullets into my hand and threw them out among the sage. I tossed the gun back to Sam. "Why don't you put this thing up."

Sam opened the door, easily this time, and dropped his gun on the front seat.

"Okay, what do you want?" I said.

"I guess you thought I wanted to kill you."

"It did kind of look that way. Can't say I blame you."

"You're gonna think I'm crazy." The circles under Sam's eyes deepened in the starlight.

"I already know you're crazy." I pointed at a large boulder in front of my Beetle. "Sit down." Sam shuffled over to the rock like a prisoner and sat down. "Why did you follow me?" I said.

Sam hesitated. "I want to know how you do those things."

I didn't say anything, just looked at him.

"Can you teach me?"

"I don't know whether I can or not. But supposing I can, why should I?"

"Maybe there's something I can do for you."

"Maybe, but it doesn't work that way. There's a price to pay for being the way I am, but not that kind of price."

"What kind of price then?"

I thought about it for a minute. I didn't know the answer.

"I've got to drive to South Carolina. Why don't you help me drive and we'll talk about it."

"You mean now?"

"Yeah, I mean right now."

"Well, I'll need to make a few calls. The Mercedes is gassed up and ready to go."

"No calls. And we go in the Bug."

Sam looked at the dilapidated VW. "But why? I mean if we have a choice."

"That *is* our choice," I said.

"But what about my car?"

"What about it?"

"And Margaret needs to know I'm not coming in. I've got to cancel appointments. I've got to appear in court on Thursday."

"Make up your mind."

"Is this the price you were talking about?"

"It's only the beginning, believe me. You're a man with a lot to lose. You should just go home and be a lawyer and forget about this."

"I can't do that." His voice sounded weak, tired. "I've got to know what's going on."

He walked over to his car and opened the trunk. Shifting his golf bag, he dug out some shirts and a pair of pants and stuffed them into a paper sack.

"Let's do it," he said with a look of relief.

I started up and began to maneuver the Beetle slowly back down the ridge. But I had to stop. My eyes struggled not only with the darkness, but with the light, threads of light connecting sage to rock to lizard to blades of yucca. The interior of the car itself was rich with a penetrating light. I realized that all I wanted to do was to be alone right there so that I could absorb it all, and be absorbed.

Something grabbed my shoulder and shook me. I loosened myself from the vision and looked into Sam's eyes.

"Do you want me to drive?" he asked.

I shook my head and continued to creep down the ridge. By the time we made it to Denver, Sam's knees were killing him, and he was having second thoughts. He made some phone calls from a gas station. Rented a room in a motel across the street. Said he was catching a bus the next day back to Colorado Springs.

THE TRIP BACK to South Carolina was grueling, but I was young then, able to sleep on the side of the road for a few hours and just keep going. I wanted to travel fast and cheap. Wanted to arrive home with as much of my own money in my pocket as possible.

In all these years I have never used the power. I've been tempted, but I've never succumbed. Not using it is a kind of discipline. Maybe it's THE discipline, for me at least. It's been so long now since I last used it on that ridge in Colorado that I don't know if I still have it. What's even stranger is that I don't know if I ever had it. I woke up one day in my father's house, and for all the world I felt like a man who could spit in the presence of other men, even though I'd done nothing in the world to prove my worthiness. I just felt it. And the power is like that too, something that I feel inside of me without understanding exactly how or why it's there. A deep humming in my bones imperceptible to anyone but myself. Did it help me catch that hammer as it fell from the edge of the roof and would have hit a member of my crew standing on the ground beneath? I don't know. Or is it that the power was one thing in my past and is now something else altogether. I don't know.

I'M SITTING HERE now, writing these last pages, in a diner outside Albuquerque, deserted except for me and the waitress doubling as cook. And one small jumping spider exploring the surface of the table. All I'm having is coffee. A motel is waiting for me a hundred miles up the road. I've been out for over three weeks this time, long hikes into what's left of the wilderness, paying attention, taking as much into myself as I can. But now I need to get back home to Rock Hill. It took me a couple of decades, but I've got a wife now, and a son, and a daughter on the way. My wife puts up with me, I don't know why. I told her I that I'd be disappearing for days at a time, and she said yes anyway, as long as she could disappear into her own solitudes from time to time. It was a good deal. I have been faithful to her, and if there's such a thing as love, then it must be what I feel for her, and for our children.

And who is this woman to whom I have been given and who has been given to me? I don't know, exactly. I can watch her at work in the kitchen, watch her playing with our son on our rough lawn, watch her sleeping serenely beside me, watch her awaken and smile, acknowledge that luxurious desire flicker in her eyes. I can take her in my arms and hold her, feel her giving her body over to my hands, that amazing trust, and I can study every inch of her body with my fingers and my lips, and still I don't know her, not exactly, not completely, so complete is her mystery.

What I said to Pheiffer was right back then, I don't need Frank or Lyuba or any of them. What would Frank do if he saw me coming, what would he say? Probably disappear in a cloud of cigarette smoke. Would Lyuba even speak to me? Are any of them still alive? I know that I am mortal, vulnerable, free, and connected in a thousand ways to everything that exists. Everything matters. Everything is real. What else could they possibly teach me?

I think I'll stop writing now. I can feel the light traveling from me in an unbreakable string to that small spider. This is not any special power. This is just the way it is. Is she aware of me? She's hungry, leaping several inches at a time in pursuit of the tiny gnats lighting on the table. Amazing. With every lunge, she strikes a spark somewhere deep inside me.

Printed in the USA
CPSIA information can be obtained
at www.ICGtesting.com
JSHW082205140824
68134JS00014B/443